"I'm Craig Adams and I'd like to sleep with you."

She forced the type of "cool" smile she'd practised at least a hundred times in the mirror and willed her voice to calmness.

"Really? Well, I'm Taylor Radcliffe and you're out of luck—I don't sleep around."

"I'm not asking you to sleep with anyone but me, Taylor Radcliffe."

"You're still out of luck," she replied, taking a sip of her drink for courage. "I'm a virgin."

"Then you'll be starting at the top!"

FROM HERE TO PATERNITY—romances that feature fantastic men who *eventually* make fabulous fathers. Some seek paternity, some have it thrust upon them. All will make it—whether they like it or not!

ALISON KELLY, a self-confessed sports junkie, plays netball, volleyball and touch football, and lives in Australia's Hunter Valley. She has three children and the type of husband women tell their daughters doesn't exist in real life! He's not only a better cook than Alison, but he isn't afraid of vacuum cleaners, washing machines or supermarkets. Which is just as well, otherwise this book would have been written by a starving woman in a pigsty!

Humor, emotion, passion...**Alison Kelly** has it all! We know you'll love the warm, witty writing style of this lively new talent for Presents.

ALISON KELLY

Yesterday's Bride

Harlequin Books

TORONTO • NEW YORK • LONDON
AMSTERDAM • PARIS • SYDNEY • HAMBURG
STOCKHOLM • ATHENS • TOKYO • MILAN
MADRID • WARSAW • BUDAPEST • AUCKLAND

FOR TRACY & BROOKE RUSSO,
THE INSPIRATION BEHIND
TAYLOR & MELANIE

ISBN 0-373-11903-8

YESTERDAY'S BRIDE

First North American Publication 1997.

Copyright © 1997 by Alison Kelly.

This edition published by arrangement with Harlequin Books S.A.

® and TM are trademarks of the publisher. Trademarks indicated with ® are registered in the United States Patent and Trademark Office, the Canadian Trade Marks Office and in other countries.

Printed in U.S.A.

PROLOGUE

AFTER returning her gaze from across the crowded yard for what seemed like an eternity, he straightened and pushed off the picket fence he'd been nonchalantly propped against and started towards her.

The current of electric excitement that rushed through her body caused her heart to lurch and the drink she held to slop over her hand. She swallowed hard, unfamiliar with the confused messages her brain and body were radiating through her. She recognized one as fear, but wasn't sure if it stemmed from the possibility he might veer off the direct course he was taking to her or that he wouldn't.

With each swaggering step the denim-and-leather-clad male took, her teenage heart beat faster, until it was drumming so fiercely it crashed into her lungs and took her breath away.

'G'day, I'm Craig Adams and I'd like to sleep with you.'

She forced the type of 'cool' smile she'd practised at least a hundred times in the mirror and willed her voice to calmness. 'Really? Well, I'm Taylor Radcliffe and you're out of luck—I don't sleep around.'

'I'm not asking you to sleep with anyone but me, Taylor Radcliffe.'

'You're still out of luck,' she replied, taking a sip of her drink for courage. 'I'm a virgin.'

'Then you'll be starting at the top.'

'But if I start at the top the only place I can go is down.'

His grin was sinful. 'See you've got the hang of it already! I like a fast learner.'

The innuendo was hardly veiled. But even as Taylor backed up against the paling, she was excited rather than afraid of the stranger's arrogant and direct pick-up technique.

'I've been warned off you by my friend,' she informed him. 'You're not considered financially desirable.'

'You, on the other hand, Taylor Radcliffe, are considered very financially desirable,' he returned, planting his hands on the fence just above her shoulder.

'Ah! So you want me for my money.'

'No. I just *want* you,' he whispered against her already opening mouth. 'For the rest of my life.'

Four months later they married. She was eighteen; he was twenty-one...

CHAPTER ONE

'*WHAT the hell have you done to your hair*?'

For five years Taylor had wondered what her estranged husband's first words would be when they met again. Yet in all her mental scenarios not once had she imagined his reaction to be outrage because she'd changed her hairstyle.

Then again, considering his opening line when they'd first met, *nothing* Craig Adams said should have surprised her. Despite the fact he was now a conservatively dressed thirty-two-year-old executive, his slow, provocative brown-eyed appraisal of her body was as brash as it had been twelve years earlier when he'd worn leather and blue jeans. And it stirred the same surge of feral excitement Taylor had hoped she'd outgrown....

'Answer me, Taylor!'

The impatient command startled her from her introspection. 'I've had it cut and permed.' At his blank look she added, '*My hair*. I've had it—'

'I'm not the slightest bit interested in your hair!' he snapped, contradicting his earlier words. 'I want to know what you're doing barging in here without an appointment!'

'*Appointment*? In case you've forgotten, I *own* half this business!'

'Hardly! I sign the bloody dividend cheques you've been receiving the past five years!'

'Keep your voice down,' she hissed. 'There's no need to shout. Melanie's in the outer office and I don't want her to hear us arguing.'

His expression was one of utter astonishment. '*Melanie*?'

'Yes. That's why I'm here. She wants you to have lunch with us.'

'*What*?'

'I asked you to stop shouting. She wants—'

'I *heard* what you said, Taylor. What I want to know is *why*.'

'Because you're her father.' She saw him physically wince at the words and hated him for it.

'She doesn't even know me!'

'That's why she wants you to have lunch with us. She wants to meet you.'

Craig moved from behind his desk to gaze dazedly at the panoramic view of Sydney Harbour, trying to marshal his confused thoughts and shell-shocked emotions into some kind of order.

Each month as he automatically wrote out the child-support cheque, he dimly acknowledged the fact that some day his daughter would probably insist on seeking him out. He'd resigned himself to the fact. But he'd also figured he wouldn't have to deal with her until at least another ten years down the track, when the kid might have had some chance of understanding how he felt. Suddenly *someday* was *today*. And it was too soon—for him *and* for Melanie.

How did you tell a five-year-old that you resented her like hell for depriving you of the only woman you'd ever loved? For stuffing up what had been a wonderful marriage? 'Struth, even his parents hadn't dumped *that* on him until he was nearly eleven! Damn Taylor! She had no right barging in here unannounced and dumping this on him! No right walking back into his life and turning it on its ear! *Yet again*.

He wheeled around and nailed her with a cold stare. 'You should have warned me about this! This isn't the sort of thing you spring on a person, Taylor!'

She knew he was right, but she'd hoped that turning up unexpectedly would make the possibility of Craig refusing to see her that much less likely. 'I guess I should have called,' she conceded. 'But Melanie wanted it to be a surprise.'

'*Melanie wanted*? I've never heard anything so ludicrous! Do you mean to tell me you flew here to pander to the whim of a kid?'

'No,' she said. 'We drove.'

'*You drove from Adelaide to Sydney so she could have lunch with me*?'

'We don't live in Adelaide any more.' She took a steadying breath, almost frightened of what his reaction to her next words would be. 'We moved back to Sydney a month ago.'

'You...you're here? *Living here*? In *Sydney*?'

If Craig's tone reflected anything other than disbelief, she could only have said it was *horror*. Disappointment nearly crushed her. Did he hate her *that* much?

'So,' he continued, again turning to the window, 'where are you living?'

It amazed Craig he could even *speak* much less ask appropriate questions. It seemed ridiculous that a day that had started out as routinely as this one had could take such a drastic turn for the *unbelievable*.

Taylor was back. Back in Sydney. Back in his life.

Closing his eyes to the scenic view and his ears to Taylor's explanation for her move east, Craig tried to get a handle on what he was feeling. But his emotions seemed like a five-thousand-piece jigsaw that had just been tipped out of its box—a jumbled, fragmented mess, bearing little resemblance to the orderly picture the pieces were supposed to form.

For two years after she'd left him, he'd started each day half expecting, half hoping she would walk into his office and say she'd made a mistake. Tell him he was the most important thing in her world and that without him she'd shrivel up and die. It wasn't an image prompted by ego or vanity; once it had been their daily litany. Then the baby had arrived and seemingly overnight everything changed....

Taylor had ceased to display even a token amount of affection towards him and she adopted a new litany—she was *too tired...too busy...Melanie needed her more than him...he had to keep the business going*! Her excuses had been boundless, pathetically transparent and signified the beginning of the end where their marriage was concerned.

At first he'd tried to fight the inevitable, and when that failed he'd tried to ignore it, but to no avail. Without warning or even an acknowledgement that their marriage was in trouble, Taylor had left him.

'Craig, are you listening? I asked—'

'I heard you,' he said wearily. 'You asked me whether I would meet with Melanie.'

He turned back to the woman to whom he'd once given his heart. Her beauty, as exquisite as ever, made him angry; her body, as streamlined as it had been at eighteen, made him hard. He swore, sitting down so the desk could at least let him keep his dignity.

'Craig, Mel doesn't know the details of...what happened.'

Her attempt at diplomacy drew a harsh laugh from his lips. 'Jeez, Taylor, I'm sure you could be more specific if you tried! Exactly what *details* are you referring to?'

His bitterness stabbed at Taylor's heart, her own urge to respond twisting the knife. She clamped her teeth shut against the pain and the cruel retort that came too easily to her tongue. She'd known this wouldn't be easy, but for Melanie's sake she wouldn't let past bitterness contaminate the present.

'I mean, Craig,' she said, forcing her voice to evenness, 'that she doesn't know you hold her responsible for what happened between us.'

'Don't *you* hold her responsible?'

'*No*,' she said with assurance. 'It was lack of trust that killed what we had, not Melanie.'

'Lack of trust, or *misplaced* trust?'

She sighed. 'You'll never believe I didn't intentionally conceive Melanie, will you?' His gaze was rigidly accusing and Taylor had to force herself not to flinch.

'No,' he responded, 'I won't.'

'No one but you, Craig, has ever called me a liar.'

'I've never used that word.'

True, but he'd made *manipulative*, *calculating* and *scheming* sound just as derogatory. Just as painful. Just as chilling. 'You implied it,' she said. 'It's the same thing.'

'Listen, Taylor,' he said through gritted teeth. 'We agreed before we got married that given our own childhood experiences, we would never have children. It was a *joint* decision and any change to that agreement should have also been a *joint* one!'

'But my getting pregnant was an *accident*!'

'You know you sound even more insistent now than you did when you first made that claim! I'd almost believe you if I didn't *remember* you casually tossing up the idea of having a family.'

'I didn't *casually toss up* anything!' she flared. 'I told you I thought that after six years of marriage, we could handle the pressures of being parents and—'

The thump of his fist on the glass-topped desk as he sprang to his feet quelled Taylor's speech.

'And when I disagreed, you said *I was right*! You *admitted* letting yourself be swayed by the fact so many of our friends were starting families! And then—' he snapped his fingers '—bingo, you're *accidentally* pregnant!'

Craig felt an old anger rising as he recalled how Taylor had venomously and repeatedly denied his accusations that she'd deliberately planned the situation; how she'd tearfully claimed she'd been taking the Pill religiously. He didn't believe her, of course, and the ensuing rows had been loud and plentiful, but since neither of them advocated abortion, Craig had resigned himself to the fact that a baby was going to encroach upon their happiness.

Taylor had sworn a child would never come between them, that it would actually bring them closer, and for a while there he'd believed her. If he were honest with himself, and surely after five years he could be that at least, there *had* been a time when he'd begun to look forward to the child's birth. Then things had started to go wrong. Now he wanted only to forget it. Only he wasn't going to be granted that wish. He turned back to the woman assigned by the devil to disrupt his ordered life.

She was beautiful. So extraordinarily, hauntingly beautiful that even after all this time he'd often wake hard with wanting her, hungry for the feel of her exquisitely sculptured body writhing in sweat beneath his. The shorter cut of her tawny hair in no way detracted from her beauty, only enhanced the long, graceful curve of her neck, making the visual progression down to her high, firm breasts all the more exciting. The short skirt she wore hugged her hips and displayed legs most men only dreamed of having wrapped around them. He wasn't immune to that dream, but the knowledge that for him it had once been reality empowered it with nightmare-like side-effects.

Though her heart pounded and her hormones were running amok in a rush of sensuality, Taylor forced herself not to squirm under Craig's slow scrutiny of her body. It wasn't easy, for even without touching her he had the power to make her ache with want. No one but him had ever possessed her body, yet she knew with certainty no one but him would ever be able to satisfy it. His hands and mouth had introduced her to pleasures she'd never imagined possible and it was difficult for her to remain focused on the purpose of her visit when she'd been deprived of such pleasures for half a decade. Heat pooled in the pit of her stomach; raw desire began building within her.

When he finally brought his eyes level with her face, the urge to go to him almost overpowered her. Only one thing held her immobile. The knowledge that passion didn't equate with trust. It was trust she wanted to see illuminate the bottomless depths of Craig's dark brown eyes.

She managed to hold his gaze for nearly a minute before eventually lowering her lashes. It was a minuscule victory, but a victory none the less. Once she'd have succumbed to his visual seduction within seconds. This time she'd met it with impunity—well, outward impunity at least.

Perhaps seeing those identical eyes in her daughter had increased her resistance, for there was no doubt Melanie was a carbon copy of her father. They shared the same almost-black hair, the same deep-set eyes and wide brow, and the same neat, flat ears. Fortunately for Melanie, though, her beautifully delicate nose had been spared being pushed slightly off-centre in a rugby brawl and a cricket bat hadn't left a scar two inches below her left eye!

Fury welled in Craig at the sight of her half smirk. 'What's so funny, Taylor?' he demanded, angry at being her source of amusement.

'I was thinking how lucky Melanie is that your nose is the result of a rugby game and not hereditary. She's the image of you, Craig,' she said softly. 'I didn't even get a look in.'

Shocked as he was by her admission, he wondered if he hadn't imagined the sadness tinging the words. So, his daughter looked like him. Funny he'd never given any thought at all to what the child might look like. Now it seemed he would be finding out firsthand.

'What's she like?' he asked.

'That's something you'll have to find out yourself. I'm biased. I think she's wonderful.'

This time her smile was full-strength pride and happiness, and having been starved of it for five years, Craig was unprepared for its potency. It put his pulse speed up and all but knocked the breath from his lungs. Strange how something as simple as a smile could practically bring a grown man to his knees, but then Taylor's had always had that effect on him. From the first time he'd seen her, he realized *her* happiness ensured *his* happiness....

Why then was he standing here contemplating meeting the person who had stolen that happiness?

About to refuse the lunch invitation, he glimpsed a flash of fear in the clear emerald eyes that studied him. What was it she feared? The past or the future? Herself or him?

'What do *you* want me to do, Taylor?' he asked.

'Me? I...'

Caught off guard by his question, she paused and took a slow breath, the rise and fall of her breasts taunting him. Gripping the sides of his chair, Craig forced his face to remain impassive.

'I want the decision to be entirely yours, just as lunch was Melanie's. What I *don't* want, Craig, is for her to be hurt.' There was a wealth of warning in her voice.

'And what,' he asked coolly, 'do you think would hurt her the most? My refusal or my acceptance?'

'Your bitterness.' There'd been no hesitation in her answer.

Amazement froze every muscle in Craig the instant he saw the child. Looking into the tiny face was like looking at a childhood photograph of himself—identical colouring and identical brown eyes.

The notion that this child was his own flesh and blood created alternate waves of terror and masculine pride within him. He had the urge to embrace her, but feared the consequences of doing so. Such an action was bound to be fraught with emotional danger although whether for him or the kid, he wasn't sure.

Though *physically* Melanie looked nothing like Taylor, Craig experienced the same sensation of uncertainty under her thorough visual inspection as he had when Taylor had looked him over from the other side of the yard twelve years ago. There was interest but no indication of whether the observer was pleased or disappointed by what they found. She had Taylor's style and panache, too, he decided, taking in the miniature hiking boots, khaki shirt and shorts, and the baseball cap worn backwards atop her long, straight hair.

The child darted a quick, uncertain look at her mother, before bringing her brown eyes back to him. Uncomfortable with the ongoing silence, Craig cleared his throat. 'Hello, Melanie.' He wasn't surprised to hear his voice lacked some of its usual confidence.

'Hello.'

The response was soft but not hesitant as she boldly stepped to within two feet of him and tilted her head back. She *was* small—barely reaching his mid-thigh.

'How tall are you?' she inquired.

Stunned to discover the kid had obviously been sizing *him* up, too, he was slow to reply. The delay earned him an impatient look.

'Don't you *know*?'

'Sure I do! I'm...six foot four.'

The child nodded and continued to silently appraise him. Craig looked to Taylor for some indication as to

what was expected of him now and was nonplussed to
see the shimmer of tears in her eyes. It had a heart-
wrenching and sobering effect. He glanced back at the
little girl.

'So,' he said, 'you want me to have lunch with you,
huh?' She nodded solemnly in response, but her steady
gaze hinted she was expecting more input from him.
'Right then ... well, er, do you like Italian food?'

'Do you?' she countered.

'Well ... yes. Yes, I do.'

'I don't.' She gave a theatrical shudder. 'I *hate* Italian
food.'

'I thought all kids liked pizza.' Craig was basing his
assumption on the fact there were always kids in pizza
commercials.

'Pizza isn't *Italian*. Pizza is normal food.'

'Normal food ...' he echoed. 'I see ...' He didn't and
looked towards Taylor for verbal backup, but her eyes
remained focused only on her daughter. He was obviously on his own. 'Well, I guess we could have pizza
for lunch if—'

'No,' the pint-size female vetoed the idea. 'I don't feel
like pizza. Know what kids *really* like?'

He shook his head. 'Believe me, I wouldn't have a
clue about—'

A childish giggle cut him off. 'What's *your* favourite
food in the whole world?'

Again she caught him mentally off stride. 'My
favourite food in the whole world?' He paused, trying
to recall if he had one. 'I guess it'd have to be grilled
barramundi.'

'Oh.' If the child's tone hadn't told him he'd again
come up with the wrong answer, her stance would have.
Her arms were folded and she was frowning at him as
if she were a teacher and he a troublesome pupil. 'You
do like McDonald's, though, don't you?' she prompted.
'*Everybody* likes McDonald's.'

Craig wasn't crazy about the direction this conversation was taking, but he had no chance to voice his objections.

'Cheeseburgers are my favourite,' Melanie told him. ''Cept *Mummy*—' her tone was scathing '—hardly ever lets me go there 'less it's for a real special reason.'

Peripherally aware of Taylor's tense stance, Craig struggled for both patience and a tactful response. 'Yes, well...I guess mothers are like that,' he said.

'Fathers aren't, though,' the child stated. 'My friend Renee's father takes her there every Friday.'

'Lucky Renee!' he muttered, earning a withering look from Taylor.

'Struth! What was he supposed to say, for God's sake? He knew zilch about kids and even less about what fathers were and weren't supposed to do. 'Well, I guess,' he said cautiously, 'it's all right on Fridays—'

'It's Friday today!'

His stomach pleaded a silent protest at the child's reaction and again he looked at Taylor. She *knew* he'd never been partial to hamburgers, not even designer ones.

'You can always have chicken nuggets,' she suggested neutrally.

'Thanks, you're a big help!' he muttered before addressing the child again. 'You're sure you wouldn't rather have something else—Chinese, French, fried chicken...'

He wondered how much vigorous shaking a kid's head could take before it actually fell off. Ah heck! How bad could it be?

'OK,' he said wearily, slinging his jacket over his shoulder. 'McDonald's it is, then.'

Across Melanie's head, Taylor mouthed the words *thank you* and gave him a smile so warm he was tempted to tell her he'd buy the kid her own franchise if Taylor would only keep looking at him like that!

Reacting to long-past memories and old habits, his hand moved inviting Taylor's into it, but she averted her gaze, and it was her daughter's hand she reached for...not his.

CHAPTER TWO

As THEY sat amid the bustle and laughter of the family-orientated restaurant, the heavy silence hanging over their table wasn't conducive to making Taylor feel comfortable. The air seemed like a volatile mix of suppressed anger, bottled-up resentment and raw sexuality, which threatened to explode at any moment. She knew if it did, her child would be the most critically injured.

It was obvious Craig was anxious to be anywhere but where he was, and Taylor resented the way her body was reacting to his reluctant presence. Why were the random memories running through her head only the kind that caused a surge of sensual adrenalin to course through her? Lord knew more than enough unpleasant scenarios had been played out between her and Craig in the later stages of their marriage. Why was it they seemed incidental now?

With the benefit of twenty-twenty hindsight, she realized it would have been better had she arranged for Melanie to meet her father alone. Her daughter was all too aware of the undertow of tension rippling beneath the stop-start conversation of the last fifteen or so minutes; it showed in her uncharacteristic quietness.

Reaching for her fries, Taylor realized they, like everything else, were now cold. But it didn't matter. Emotionally she'd been too wound up to eat; only for Mel's sake had she made an effort. Yet considering how every time she lifted her eyes from her food, she'd encountered rich brown masculine ones that negated her ability to chew, swallow or execute any of the automatic

19

steps of eating, she didn't think she'd convinced anyone she was enjoying the meal.

'Not hungry?' Craig asked. She gave a tight smile and shook her head. His eyes skimmed over her face as if taking an inventory of her features, then with a seductive smile he helped himself to her half-eaten burger. 'I am.'

Without taking his eyes from hers, he bit slowly into the same spot she had. Remembering how those even white teeth had felt nibbling on her flesh, she felt her stomach somersault as a wave of heat rose from her toes into her cheeks. *Oh, hell*! *This was insane*!

'What about you, Mel?' Craig was asking. 'Would you like something else?'

'No, thank you.'

He frowned, then reached for his wallet. 'Sure you wouldn't like to go buy yourself an ice cream or something?' he urged.

Melanie cast a concerned look at him, then quickly lowered her eyes and shook her head. 'No, thank you,' she said again.

Her daughter's lifeless response prompted Craig to send Taylor a *what's wrong with her?* look.

Annoyed at his pseudo-innocence, she sent him a furious *well, what do you expect?* glare in return. Why wouldn't the poor kid have clammed up? Taylor fumed silently. He'd practically ignored her since they'd left the office! He'd been so busy studying *her*, Melanie could have sprouted wings and flown away and he wouldn't have noticed! It didn't matter that *she* had been more than a little preoccupied with less than motherly thoughts. After all, Melanie could have lunch with her *any time*. Craig was here at Mel's request; the least he could do was be attentive to her.

Not that she owed him any favours, Taylor told herself, but for Melanie's sake she'd better give him some direction if this lunch wasn't going to turn into an even bigger disaster than it already was! Ensuring her daughter wasn't watching, she pointed first at Craig, then at her own mouth and finally at Melanie. Then she opened her hand in imitation of a duck quacking to indicate Craig should say something to the child.

It took a couple of seconds before comprehension dawned on Craig's handsome features.

What? he mouthed back.

Anything! she returned.

I don't know what to say to her! Craig enunciated each word silently. Damn, he thought, it was all very well for Taylor to look at him as if he was a complete moron when it came to children, but he'd *never* had to deal with them. *She'd* never given him the chance! He glanced at the small dark head beside him, seeking inspiration, but none came. How could a businessman of his calibre be so devoid of something appropriate to say? Why, when he'd rescued deals with some of the most high-powered men in the world, was he being awestruck by a pint-size kid?

His attention again became focused on Taylor. Mouth pursed, she looked daggers at him, then again started to speak voicelessly. The silent movement of her lips and the hint of tongue and teeth revealed by her actions stirred heat in his loins. Cursing mentally, he shifted in his seat, trying to concentrate on what she was mouthing to him, rather than on her delicious mouth.

Dammit! He couldn't make out what the last word was. He sent her a blank look and watched intently as she mouthed her message again.

Ask her about . . . Hell! He still couldn't make it out.

'She said, "Ask her about school".'

Guiltily, both adults looked at the owner of the tiny voice. Obviously the child had intercepted her mother's message to him and interpreted it better than him.

'Er. . . yes. How is school? Do you like it?' he asked woodenly.

'I don't know,' the little girl responded. 'I haven't started yet.'

Taylor blushed under Craig's stinging glare. 'I...I only enrolled her today. She starts next week. At St Catherine's. My old school. It has a junior school as well as high school. Mel's going to the junior school.'

'I'm sure I'd have assumed the high school if you hadn't pointed that out,' he said drily.

'I'm not old enough for high school—' Melanie again stopped short and pondered the man beside her. 'What should I say?' she asked both adults.

Taylor frowned. 'About what, darling?'

'To finish talking to *him*.'

Unsure exactly what her daughter was on about, Taylor hedged. 'Um...what do you think you should say...to finish talking to him?'

The little girl wore a considering expression for a few moments then delivered a direct gaze to the man beside her. 'Is *Daddy* okay?'

Taylor's gasp was nothing compared to the half-strangled gurgle Craig emitted and one look was enough to tell her *Daddy* wasn't okay. His face was drained of all colour and he looked as if he'd been poleaxed!

'I...I'm fine. I think,' he muttered, reefing at his already-loose tie.

'No, I mean do you want me to call you Daddy or Craig or mister or sir or...?'

The kid was counting off the various titles on her fingers, but Craig had no idea how to answer her. 'Er...well—' he paused and tried to gather his thoughts '—maybe you should ask Taylor...I mean your mother...Mummy...'

'This is something you two should decide between yourselves,' Taylor responded quickly.

In that instant, Craig was swamped by a dozen emotions, all generated by the woman sitting opposite him. Passion was easily the most dominant one, but he wasn't sure whether it would be best purged by reaching across and kissing her or reaching across and *choking* her. In view of her amused grin, he fancied the latter.

'Well?' Melanie pressed. 'What do you want me to call you?'

Slowly he turned to the child. For a little girl, she certainly had a big attitude, he decided, amused by her arched eyebrow. He stiffened, knowing the same had been said of him as a kid. He felt his heart swell—*his daughter*. His own flesh and blood. He was both humbled and proud to think she resembled him so closely.

'Daddy sounds pretty good to me,' he said, clearing his throat when his words sounded a bit scratchy. 'It'll probably take us both a bit of time to get used to it, though,' he told her.

'It'll be easy for me!' Melanie proclaimed, her wide smile reflecting in her eyes. 'I'm used to talking to your picture and calling you Daddy.'

'*My picture*?'

'Yeah, the one Mummy keeps on her dressing table.'

Craig raised an eyebrow and studied his estranged wife. 'Now, that's *interesting*.'

Taylor could have cheerfully throttled her beloved daughter on the spot but she managed a careless shrug. 'It's important for children to identify with a father figure,' she said. 'I don't believe in telling horror stories about absent parents. So I just omit the gory bits!'

'So why not keep it on Melanie's dressing-table?'

'Because there's no room on it! It's already chock-a-block with her favourite stuffed animals.'

Melanie stood up. 'I'm going to the toilet.'

'*Again*? You went at the office.' Taylor almost groaned on hearing her inane response. Melanie was old enough to decide when she needed to relieve herself! The truth was she was uncomfortable with the thought of being left alone with Craig. 'Do you want me to come with you?' she asked hopefully.

The five-year-old rolled her eyes. 'Mummy, I'm not a baby!'

'Frightened to be alone with me, Taylor?' Craig's sexy drawl, coated in amusement, came on the heels of Melanie's departure.

Taylor ignored the remark. At twenty-nine, she hoped she was sophisticated enough to deal with her feelings for Craig Adams. Now she wondered if she wasn't every bit as naïve as she'd been when she left him five years earlier. Around this man her emotions always seemed to bamboozle her common sense. Nothing, it seemed, had changed. *But there was no reason he had to know that.* From here on she'd treat him like any other male acquaintance—with polite pleasantness, nothing more.

'So...' She hoped he didn't notice the breathy sound of her voice. 'How's the business doing?'

'You can't tell from the size of the dividend cheques?'

'I didn't mean financially. I was curious about what sort of expansions we've made.'

'*We've* made?' He scowled. 'Listen, Taylor, you've been a silent partner in this firm for the best part of six years. Don't think you can waltz back here and start quizzing me on how I run the company!'

'I...I never meant to imply...' She paused and tried again. 'I was only making conversation—'

'Ah! Sorry I didn't realize your interest was only superficial!'

'It's not!' she protested, angry at his accusation. Once Adams Relief had been as much the focus of her life as his. When they'd started the temporary-staffing business, a year after their marriage, they'd only listed replacement office staff on their books, but within eight months they had several highly qualified people capable of stepping into managerial positions. Three years from the inception of the business, Craig had seen an opportunity for expansion. Himself a qualified mechanic who'd completed his business-management degree at night, he saw the need for qualified tradesmen to be provided on a relief basis and so Adams Relief stretched its services to cater for this demand, also.

Taylor had to admit that for a long time, like Craig, she had regarded Adams Relief as their 'child' and had delighted in watching it grow and develop under their guidance. But unexpectedly her maternal instincts started to surface and she became less and less satisfied with the idea of being solely career orientated. Craig, however, had been so completely opposed to amending their original decision to never have children, Taylor hadn't raised the issue a second time and pushed the idea from her mind. At least she tried.

Perhaps it was some sort of trick of her subconscious that allowed her to fall pregnant. Perhaps it was a case of wishing too hard and too often, but regardless of what quirk of nature saw her get pregnant while using contraceptives, the fact was she did.

Thinking of her precious daughter, she was eternally grateful the decision had been taken from her hands.

'Rest assured, Craig,' she said, 'I have no desire to try to interfere with the way you've been running the firm.'

'Too busy overseeing the Radcliffe family fortunes, are we?'

'I won't even dignify that remark with an answer!'

'You're right. That was uncalled for.' He presented her with an apologetic look. 'I really was sorry to hear about your parents. A hotel fire is a tragic way to die. It can't have been easy for you to deal with.'

'I coped. And at least they went together.' She gave a small ironic smile. 'I doubt either of them could have survived without the other. Or wanted to.'

Craig recognized the flash of pain in her face. He knew that as a child, Taylor had spent her life on the outside, looking in at parents too wrapped up in themselves to notice their little girl. She'd always claimed if she ever loved anyone as completely as her parents loved each other, she'd never have children. Six years into their marriage, she'd changed her mind.

'They were quite different once my father retired and Mel and I moved to Adelaide,' she said softly as if reading his thoughts. 'Father especially was quite taken with Melanie, and Mother showed me dozens of albums full of photographs of me as a baby.' She gave a brittle laugh. 'Of course, there aren't many of me from the age of five onwards. Boarding-schools aren't big on taking snaps of pupils.'

'So how come you're so keen to send Melanie to St Catherine's?'

'Because it's an excellent school.'

'Well, I think she's far too young for boarding-school—'

'*You* think!' Taylor practically spat the words. 'For your information, she'll be a day pupil not a boarder! And besides,' she said tersely, 'you've been a *silent partner* where Mel's concerned for the past five years! I've managed to make all the right decisions thus far—'

'Have you?' His interjection was ignored.

'And I don't need your two cents' worth now!'

'I'm back!' The reappearance of Melanie interrupted them.

'Good girl,' Taylor said, rising to her feet and gathering up her handbag, 'because we have to leave now.'

'Ohhh.' The protest was the universal whine of a five-year-old. Taylor ignored it not because of anything she'd read in a good-parenting manual, but because self-preservation demanded she end this fiasco as quickly as possible.

Craig caught her by the elbow. 'Have dinner with me tonight.' It wasn't a question but his tone stopped it short of being a command.

'Can we, Mummy?' Melanie pleaded, tugging Taylor's hand.

'I'm sorry, but I play basketball on Friday nights,' Taylor said, grateful for the excuse.

'You *still* play basketball?'

'I happen to believe in staying in shape and keeping fit.'

'Well,' he whispered, 'there's no denying you're in great shape, but I'd like to test out your fitness for myself. How about tomorrow night, say eight o'clock?' He smiled at her blushing confusion.

'Nnnoo...I don't like to have Melanie out late two nights in a row,' she said, dislodging his grip and hurrying to the street. He kept pace with her.

'I wasn't suggesting you bring Melanie,' he muttered.

If she'd hoped the fresh air would help clear her mind and soothe her jumbled nerves, she was wrong. The warm, early-February breeze seemed determined to sweep the musky scent of his favourite aftershave into her nostrils and into every cell of her memory. Sensual panic rushed through her, partly created by his scent and the tone of his voice, and partly by the feel of his breath on her neck. Her stride faltered and he grasped her elbow with lightning reflexes to prevent her stumbling. She jerked free as if scalded.

'I...I can't get a sitter. I've lost touch with most of my old friends,' she said.

'Even your old school pal, Dr Liz O'Shea?'

'Liz plays on the team with me when she's not on duty.'

'Well, then, hire a professional.' Her look of outraged horror told Craig he'd made a tactical mistake.

'I *will not* leave Melanie with strangers! The answer is *no*!'

He shoved his hands into his pockets, pondering the idea of hauling her into his arms and kissing her into agreement, but one look at her determined features crushed the egotistical belief he could do it. But he wasn't prepared to let her walk away without knowing for sure he was going to see her again. Soon.

He was struggling with a solution when he caught sight of the childish smile being beamed up at him. Well, he thought, returning the little girl's grin, *All's fair in love and war*.

'Hey, Melanie,' he said, 'how would you feel if I called over one night next week to check how you were doing at school?'

'Craig!' Taylor's blurted anger was drowned out by her daughter.

'Wow, that'd be great! You could have dinner with us!'

'Now *there's* a great idea!' He patted the child's head, his eyes on Taylor. 'I'm free Monday,' he said, finding the fury in her green eyes nostalgic.

'Monday's no good! Mel will be too tired after her first day at school.'

'That's okay,' he said. 'Tuesday's equally good for me.'

'Tuesday she has ballet!'

'There's always Wednesday—'

'No, there isn't!' she said triumphantly. 'I have basketball practice until seven.'

'We'll make it after seven, then,' Craig countered, his hands balling into frustrated fists in his pockets.

'Er...no, I...'

'Say seven forty-five?'

'I...I...um...I—'

'Oh, *please*, Mummy? *Pretty please*?'

Melanie's beseeching look and misty eyes tugged at Taylor's maternal instincts while Craig's arrogant smirk pushed at her violent streak. Great! She had a choice between a confrontation with the devil in Craig and a crying jag to rival the deep blue sea from Melanie. She could either score points for herself or break her daughter's heart.

Her resigned sigh and half-hearted nod sent such a tide of relief rushing through Craig that he knew he was smiling like an idiot. 'Thanks, Taylor, I'd love to come.'

Her response was a murderous look and he was relieved to have the kid nudge his leg to gain his attention.

'Aren't you gonna thank me, too?' she asked him.

'Eh, well sure,' he said, crouching to put himself on the same level as the girl. The small arm that snaked out and hooked around his neck in an instinctively trusting action caught him off guard. He quickly lifted his eyes to the woman who had conceived this child against his wishes, seeking her guidance as to what was expected of him. But she'd turned away.

'Well, Melanie...' He paused, still at a loss as to what to say to the owner of the huge smile and innocent brown eyes fixed on him. 'I...eh...thanks for lunch. And...and I guess I'll see you Wednesday.' Quickly he set her away from him and stood up.

Blinking the blur from her eyes, Taylor made a production of looking for her car keys, hoping he'd say a quick goodbye and leave.

'Taylor?'

She lifted her head impatiently. 'Yes?'

'She seems a nice kid.'

He was so close she could count the rate of the pulse in his neck. Traitorously her mind recalled how quickly passion accelerated that pulse, how it had felt to have it throbbing beneath her tongue as she licked the sweat of lovemaking from the skin covering it.

'What's your address?'

From her body's reaction to his voice, he could have been asking her to strip. Goose bumps carpeted her skin, her own pulse went into a tailspin and her vocal cords seemed paralysed—along with every other part of her his eyes touched. It became a mental struggle to recall where she lived and her voice trembled slightly when she finally told him.

Taking hold of her wrist and softly brushing his thumb over it, he murmured, 'Sure you're not free beforehand?'

For Taylor the temptation to say *to hell with basketball* was almost overwhelming. She swallowed hard before answering in case the wild idea verbalized itself. 'Seven forty-five Wednesday,' she said firmly, removing her hand from his grasp.

'I'll be there.'

'Melanie will be looking forward to it.'

'She won't be the only one, will she, Tay?'

Tay! No one but him had ever called her that. His use of it now was intended as a deliberate reminder of shared intimacies. Ha! As if she'd needed reminding.

He uttered no other farewell, and, determined she wouldn't, either, Taylor took Melanie's hand and walked away. The child twisted, waving cheerfully to the tall, darkly handsome stranger who was her father.

'I think he likes me, Mummy,' she said proudly, buckling her seat-belt. 'Why else would he ask if he could come and visit me next week?' she mused aloud.

Why? thought Taylor, revving the car with more vigour than was necessary. Because, dammit, he used you as a means to see me! And heaven help me, I let him do it!

CHAPTER THREE

AFTER an hour of torture at the hands of old memories, Taylor sprang from her bed and slipped into her robe. The silk was cool against her heated skin and she descended the stairs wishing she could at least *pretend* the summer heat was the cause of her restlessness and inability to sleep. But knowing she'd find no reprieve in wishful thinking, she crossed the moonlit family room to the bar.

She reached for the bottle of tequila knowing alcohol cured nothing and that two previous encounters with the potent Mexican liquor had proven she and it incompatible. But desperate times called for desperate measures, and since she'd never taken sleeping pills in her life, booze was her last resort. Unscrewing the lid on the bottle, she poured what amounted to roughly a triple shot of the alcohol, then, deciding that was *too* desperate a measure, trickled half back into the bottle. For a moment she pondered the idea of adding ice.

'Oh, great, Taylor!' she muttered, recalling how Craig in their first year of marriage had set a precedent, which had made ice a special treat for hot summer nights like this one. 'Ice cubes are the *last* thing you should be thinking about!'

Determinedly she downed the straight tequila, shuddering when she lowered the glass and dreading the thought of how her head would ache in the morning. Yet the prospect of the blissful oblivion the alcohol would induce overrode all the other negative factors. Even an almost paralysing hangover was preferable to

31

the achingly arousing thoughts that had been dominating her mind since lunch.

Back upstairs, she crawled between her lilac sheets praying the effects of the alcohol would rapidly overpower both her sleeplessness and the sensual memories invading her head.

The heat gave the air the consistency of marshmallows, sapping a person of all energy, and she half wished she was back in the air-conditioned luxury of her parents' bayside home. So much had changed in the past six months, she more than anyone or anything and far more than she would ever have imagined. In the midst of tossing to free herself of the sheet twisting around her lower body, she started as something cool and moist brushed her cheekbone.

Drowsy confusion continued to fog her mind as the slippery coldness edged down along her jaw and across her bottom lip. Instinctively her tongue sought to identify the cause. It tasted cold, hard wetness and warm male flesh. She quivered, a ribbon of pleasure fluttering through her.

'Craig...' Her voice emerged as a breathy query, yet her body's sensual reaction confirmed his identity even before he spoke.

'You expecting someone else to slip into your bed tonight?'

She shook her head at the amused, raspy-voiced question, opening her eyes to the utterly male smile she adored. Yet not even the smile was enough to stop her gaze from straying down over his muscled chest, firm abdomen and slim hips. Her throat, constricting at the sight of his nude, muscular perfection, emitted a sound of feral admiration that made him grin.

'Missed me, huh?' he asked smugly.

His lips sought her mouth, giving her no chance of verbal response, but hell yes, she'd missed him! Her arms clamped tightly around his neck; they'd been parted mere hours, yet she'd missed him with an intensity she'd thought would kill her.

'I didn't expect to see you until the end of the week,' she said when they broke apart, dazed as much by his unexpected presence as the effects of his kiss.

'I know, but I was worried about you.'

'*Worried*? You don't think I can last *three days* without you?'

Chucking her indignantly jutted chin, he grinned. 'It wasn't the *days* that concerned me. I know how much trouble you have sleeping in summer, so I decided I'd better be here to keep you cool.'

Stifling a smile, she raised an eyebrow. 'Of course it was solely *my* best interests you had at heart.'

'Yeah.' He all but purred the word, and, taking what she now recognized to be an ice cube, he drew it around her hairline to the pulse behind her ear.

'Feel good?' he asked, his gaze intense.

'It feels great, but it's not going to work,' she told him. 'You're only making me hotter...' Her words died to a sigh as the frozen cube was trailed down her throat and across her chest.

'Hot, babe?' he whispered, manoeuvring the cool wetness into the valley of her breasts, then mopping it up with his tongue. 'How hot?'

Arousal flamed in her and Taylor gripped the sheets in an effort to stay centred.

'Tell me how hot I make you,' he urged. 'Better yet—' he paused only until her eyes lifted to his, then straddled her with slow, easy grace '—*show* me.'

As he said the words, the cube made contact with her nipple, sending her bucking from the mattress. Desire seared her bones as furiously as his hardness branded her belly. She made a futile grab for him but in one smooth motion he snared her wrists and stretched her arms above her head.

'Easy, honey, I'm not through cooling you.'

The taste and temperature of his kiss had Taylor equating hell with the North Pole, and as passion engulfed her, she wondered if a person could drown in fire, or combust from love. Dimly she became aware of his reaching for another ice cube from the tray by the bed, but nothing in her wildest dreams had prepared her for what he did with it.

Placing it between his teeth, he began guiding it from the base of her throat along the length of her, the combination of her overheated skin and his breath creating melting rivulets that trickled along the ridges of her ribcage as slowly as he flowed down her body. With both her blood and flesh growing more heated by the moment, each time Craig replaced one spent ice cube with a cooler, fresher one, Taylor expected to hear it sizzle as it met her skin and evaporated on contact. By the time his trail of torture reached her navel, her breathing was as ragged and erratic as the reactionary tremors that surfaced across her belly, but erupted from a far deeper core.

Millimetre by erotically slow millimetre, he orally steered the ice lower and lower until her nerve endings were ablaze to the point where she thought she would explode into a zillion pieces without ever finding the completion she craved. Her experience with this man's torrid sensuality meant there was no question as to why the ice didn't feel cold against the most sensitive part of her femininity. Every pulse in her body was screaming at sound-barrier pitch for release and her hips lifted with wanton demand for its delivery.

She was almost frantic with need for him when his dexterous mouth and hands stilled. Tossing her head, she writhed beneath him. 'Now!' she cried. 'Don't stop...*now*!'

'Look at me, Tay....' His words were breathless and strained, but the touch of his hand on her forehead signified their importance.

Forcing her lashes open, she stared at up the sweat-drenched male perfection poised above her and her heart almost exploded at the depth of emotion shining from his eyes into hers.

'I love you, Tay. I love you more than you'll ever believe. And nothing will ever change that.'

'Oh...Crai—'

His mouth claimed hers in a humid, hungry kiss that she never had a chance of controlling. Then he eased away and, with a smug, satisfied smile, moved his hips intimately against her. 'Now?' he asked.

'Yes, yes...now. *Now*...'

Taylor struggled to shrug free of the hand shaking her shoulder. It wasn't Craig's hand...it was too small. Too fragile...

'*Mummy*! *Mummy, wake up*! *You're having a bad dream*!'

Panting for breath and blinking against the glare of the bedside lamp, Taylor tried to sit up. To speak. To ignore the fact she was quaking with unsatisfied desire. To comprehend what the wide-eyed child hovering by her bed was doing in her and Craig's tiny apartment in the middle of the night.

'It's okay, Mummy,' the dark-haired child assured her. 'You must have been dreaming about being on Grandpa's farm.' She giggled. 'You kept yelling "Cow! Cow!"'

Reality struck with a crippling blow, catapulting Taylor from past pleasures to present pain. It hurt her to breathe, nearly killed her to think. Acid tears burned her eyes and throat. Tears for what she'd lost with the only man she'd ever loved and for what she'd gained with her daughter. *His daughter*.

'Mummy, if you want, I could get in bed with you so you aren't scared any more.'

Taylor pulled her daughter into a fierce hug, silent tears scalding paths down her face and her body trembling, as despair clawed her heart.

What had happened to them? What the hell had happened to the all-consuming love they'd shared? And when, dear lord, when would she stop feeling its loss?

It was well after midnight before Craig had the luxury of removing his tie and stretching out in his favourite reclining chair. He sighed wearily, lifting the glass of bourbon to his lips and savouring its soothing warmth.

His dinner meeting had gone on far longer than he'd anticipated or wanted. He allowed himself a smile as he ruefully admitted that part of the reason had been his inability to keep his mind on what was being discussed. If Taylor had consented to seeing him tonight, he'd have cancelled the engagement without a second thought. Considering the way the events of the day had distracted him from the business at hand, he would have been best served to have done so, regardless! His mind had been constantly sidetracked from the topic under discussion by images of a beautiful, green-eyed, honey-haired woman.

Taylor was back. Sexier and more beautiful than ever. And with her she'd brought a small, almost porcelain fragile, child who by rights should never have survived beyond a few days of life. He shivered as an image of his daughter's face imprinted itself in his mind. *His daughter*. The reason Taylor had walked out on him.

He took another sip of his drink, wondering if the confused emotions he felt towards the child were genuine or simply a side-effect of those he felt for her mother. And what exactly was he feeling?

Guilt? Yeah. Well, sure. He'd always felt he'd failed Taylor in some way from the moment she'd suggested they consider having a child, but suddenly the guilt felt different. Fresher, more biting.

His anger was nothing new; it had remained just below the surface of his day-to-day existence for the past five years. He'd never been sure if the bulk of it was directed at Taylor for walking out or himself for letting her. He also allowed himself to admit that until today a huge chunk of it had been focused on Melanie.

Melanie. Until scant hours ago, he'd rarely thought of the child and *never* by name. It had been the easiest way of managing the gut-wrenching jealousy that consumed him. *Jealousy*.

God! Yet *another* ugly emotion he'd fallen victim to, made worse by the fact it had been directed towards a tiny premature baby. The notion left a sick taste in his mouth and he quickly poured himself another drink, tossing it down in one gulp. Sighing, he contemplated the empty glass. For five years his life had been equally empty. Ever since the love Taylor always claimed was exclusively his had been redirected.

If she'd turned her affection to another man, Craig knew he'd have fought tooth and nail to win her back; he was cocky enough to believe no *man* was capable of taking her from him. But he hadn't counted on losing her to a baby. How did a grown man compete with a helpless child? Of course, back then he'd never really tried to compete; shattered by the discovery he'd been relegated to a distant second on Taylor's list of priorities, it had been easier to simply let her go.

And now? Well, now she was back. He didn't delude himself it was because she loved *him*—oh, no. It was maternal love that had prompted her to introduce him to his daughter. And neither did he delude himself he could forgive her for deliberately falling pregnant, but he sure as hell intended to make amends for the way he'd held the child responsible for what had happened between them.

There was an unaffected honesty about Melanie that intrigued him and he had little doubt he'd grow to like the child. To be honest, he hoped she'd grow to like him, too, for reasons other than the fact he was her father. But he knew he had no love to give his daughter;

her mother had that and she always would. It was his trust Taylor had forfeited.

He might never have wanted to be a father, but he sure as hell was going to be one *now*.

Strangely, having made that decision eased some of the tension from his body. Then again, he thought drily, perhaps it was simply the Jack Daniel's kicking in. Pouring another glass, he forced his mind to that part of his life he normally only confronted in nightmares—*The Past*. . . .

In the sterile surrounds of the hospital waiting room, Craig's hand shook as he took the polystyrene cup from Taylor's closest friend, Liz O'Shea. Emotional turmoil made him oblivious to the hot liquid that spilled onto his hand.

'*Why*, Liz? *Why* did she have to go and put herself at risk like this? I never wanted or needed a baby. She knew that! But I can't live without her. I can't live without *Taylor*!'

'Craig, her doctor is the best. She's in good hands. There's not a thing on God's earth you can do now except wait.'

It had seemed like a lifetime later that Craig looked up and saw the obstetrician striding towards them.

'Well?' he demanded of the older man. 'Where is she? What's happened?'

'She's resting, Mr Adams. But things aren't good.'

'What do you mean, *aren't good*? If anything—'

'Mr Adams, your wife is in labour.'

'But it's too early!'

'Taylor has a condition called placenta previa, caused by—'

'I don't give a stuff what it's called or what causes it! I want to know if she's going to be all right!'

'I expect so, yes. But your wife is going to have to remain here. It's the baby we need to concern ourselves with—'

'Forget the baby! It's Taylor I care about. You put *her* first!' He grabbed the front of the doctor's coat. 'You understand me? It's Taylor who's important here!'

'For heaven's sake, Craig! Pull yourself together and *listen*!' Liz urged, shaking his arm.

Realizing what he was doing, Craig released the doctor's coat and stepped away.

'I...I'm sorry, Doctor. It's just that if anything happened...'

The doctor's face relaxed. 'Believe me, I do understand.'

'So,' Craig said wearily, 'what's the bottom line in all this?'

'Your wife is in labour at twenty-five weeks along. Far, far too early. However, if we can keep the baby at bay until even twenty-seven weeks, I'll be a lot happier. I've made arrangements to have the baby transferred to the hospital with the best antenatal facilities in the city as soon as it's born. But I'll be honest with you. Even then, the child's chances of survival aren't good.'

'Taylor is your first priority,' Craig reminded him.

From then on, Craig haunted the hospital, going home only to shower, change and snatch a few hours' sleep. Twice more he had to stand helplessly by as Taylor again went into labour despite all the drugs administered to forestall such occurrences and the millions of dollars' worth of equipment monitoring both her and her unborn child. He watched, too, as she endured painful steroid injections aimed at accelerating the unborn child's lung capacity, physically flinching when agony distorted her beautiful face and squeezed tears from her exhaustion-glazed eyes. When he voiced his feelings about how much it hurt him to watch her suffer, Taylor gave a weak smile and clutched his hand.

'Darling, every bit of prodding, poking and pain is worth it, if it delays delivery. The doctors said if I can hang in for two more weeks, our baby will have a much better chance of surviving.' Fierce determination lit her weary features. 'I'm going to do it, Craig. I *have* to.'

And she did, *just*. Exactly fourteen days after her admission, Taylor went into labour for the final time, haemorrhaging heavily, but Craig wasn't with her, and by the time he reached the hospital, Taylor was undergoing an emergency Caesarean, and a short time later he learned he was the father of a three-month-premature baby girl.

He rushed straight to Taylor expecting to find her still recovering from the effects of the anaesthetic, but was shocked to learn only a spinal block had been administered and that she'd been conscious throughout the operation. Yet joy made Taylor oblivious to his anger about the procedure.

'Craig, she's so beautiful! So very, very beautiful!'

At the obvious awe in her voice, he felt a stab of rage; having seen the child, she would find its death that much harder to bear. Taylor seemed totally unaware of what was bound to happen.

'Oh, darling! She's only nine inches long but wait till you see her! She's perfect! She even cried *all by herself*! Not many babies that early can!' Taylor's voice was as bright with pride as her eyes were with tears and Craig had to swallow hard before speaking.

'I know, honey,' he said. 'But how are *you* feeling? That's what I want to know.'

'I'm great!' she responded, ashen face and sunken cheeks refuting her words. 'But don't worry about that! Go and see your daughter!'

'I will. Later. Right—'

'No, Craig, *now*! She's being transferred to one of the larger hospitals. One with better facilities.'

'Okay, I'll go,' he said, wanting to pacify her. 'But I'll be back here quick smart, so don't go anywhere!' he teased, brushing his hand gently along her cheek.

Taylor smiled and shook her head. 'They want to baptize her here before she's moved...I'd like to call her Melanie Brooke. Is that all right with you?'

He nodded. 'Sure, honey. Melanie Brooke is fine,' he replied, feeling he was making promises he couldn't keep.

Taylor received daily videos of her daughter from the hospital the child was transferred to, right up until she was discharged a week later with the proviso she take things extremely slowly. Despite the doctors' warnings, she insisted on spending eighteen-hour days with her daughter, ignoring Craig's pleas for her to get some rest, to spend more time at home, more time with him. Taylor obsessively followed her own agenda. So it was a pleasant surprise when one Saturday, while he was going over some work he'd brought home, she walked into the study in the middle of the afternoon.

'You're home early.'

She slumped wearily onto the sofa. 'I'm going back later.'

Craig crouched before her, stroking her hair and her pale, fatigue-etched face. 'I've got a better idea. Why don't you rest for a couple of hours, then we can go out for a romantic dinner, followed by dancing and—?'

Recoiling from his touch, she shrieked, 'Dancing! My daughter stopped breathing today and you expect me to go dancing?'

'Taylor! I had no idea...I'm sorry!'

She leaped to her feet, rage energizing her. 'Sorry! *Sorry*! Craig, you're probably only sorry that they *revived* her!'

'Honey, that's not true!'

'Good!' she screeched through her tears. 'Because Melanie isn't going to die! She's tough! Like *me*! She's not a *quitter* like her father! She won't die! I won't let her. I tell her that every day....'

'Tay, honey, you have to be prepared for the worst.' He reached for her, but she jumped away as if fearing contamination.

'You're a quitter, Craig Adams! I hate you!' She was beyond reasoning with. 'You never wanted a baby and the first time you saw this one you decided she was too small and too weak to survive, and that suited you! Well, she *will* survive! You hear me? She *will*!'

The strain between them from that point on became unbearable and Craig felt her drifting farther and farther away from him. In an effort to hang on to some semblance of the life they'd once shared, he threw himself into their business with maniacal ferocity. He even tried to establish a deal with the biggest staffing agency in Japan as he and Taylor had once wistfully discussed doing. But Taylor wasn't interested in talking about it, about *anything*. She rarely even mentioned the baby to him, and when she did, it was always '*my* daughter, *my* Melanie'.

The final most bitter blow came when he arrived back from a three-day trip to Tokyo, which Taylor had insisted he take despite his reluctance to leave her. He'd walked into a silent house to discover an envelope with his name on it. Its handwritten contents read:

Dear Craig,

The doctors have said Melanie is well enough to leave hospital now so I'm taking my daughter home. Since you always believed I trapped you into fatherhood, I've decided to set you free—I think this is best, not just for us, but for Melanie.

I'm going to stay with my parents in Adelaide. You can contact me there to sort out whatever legal things have to be done about the business. But since the business was always more your 'baby' than mine, I know it's better off with you, just as Melanie is better off with me.

There was no signature, but then none had been needed.

Now, nursing an empty bottle and a potential hangover, Craig wondered if five years later there was anything left to salvage between Taylor and him.

CHAPTER FOUR

'YOU stupid, great useless animal!' Taylor muttered as the huge, lumbering St Bernard raced to beat her up the stairs. 'I'm not going to bed! I'm only getting changed!'

'You better hurry,' Melanie advised from the floor of the family room. 'Daddy'll be here in *seven* minutes.'

Taylor forced a smile. Like she needed reminding! Mel had been acting like the countdown voice for Mission Control ever since they'd got home from basketball practice. She on the other hand had been hoping for a phone call from Craig saying he had to cancel.

Glancing across at her daughter carefully colouring a picture intended for Craig, Taylor instantly regretted her selfish thoughts. It was important to Melanie that her father come—vitally important. She bit her lip as doubts that had kept her sleepless since she'd arrived back in Sydney assailed her yet again.

Had she done the right thing in coming back and practically forcing Craig to acknowledge Melanie's existence? Even more disturbing was the question that had kept her awake each night since she'd walked into his office. *Had she really come for her daughter's sake, or was she simply using Melanie as an excuse to get Craig back into her own life?*

Melanie called her and held up the drawing she'd been working on. 'I tried to stay inside the lines. Do you like it?' she asked.

'Yeah! I think it's great!' Taylor replied.

'It's for Daddy to put in his office. Think *he'll* like it?'

'I'm *sure* he will.'

44

Realizing she was still in her bathrobe, her hair wet, and wasting time, she hurried up the stairs. *Would* Craig see any merit in the less than artistic scribbling of a five-year-old?

'He'd better!' she said, sliding open her wardrobe. 'Or he'll *wear* the meal he all but invited himself to!' And *that* was something she meant to have out with him. His manipulative use of Melanie was inexcusable!

After extracting a simple white flared ankle-length dress in embroidered cotton, she tossed it onto the bed, next to the sleepy-looking dog now sprawled across it.

'There, Bernie,' she said. 'No one could accuse me of dressing to impress! In fact,' she added smugly, 'I'm not even going to bother putting on make-up.'

Sitting on the bed, she plugged in the blow-drier and began drying her hair, but even the appliance's droning hum didn't drown out her daughter's excited yell. 'He's here!'

Pulse skittering, Taylor dropped the drier and jumped to her feet. *Already? Dammit, she wasn't ready!*

Craig owned up to more than a touch of apprehension as he climbed out of his car. He'd been sweating on this night for five days and now it was here he wasn't sure he was ready for it. He didn't know what to expect, or more importantly, what was expected *of* him.

As he made his way up the path, the front door opened and Melanie stood waiting for him.

'Hello,' she said, offering a smile.

'G'day, Melanie,' he said, then wondered if it was acceptable to hand a bottle of wine to a five-year-old. He was still considering this when she tugged at his arm and led him from the tiled entrance foyer into a modern, comfortably furnished lounge.

'What's in the bag?' she asked.

'A bottle of wine.'

'I'll put it in the 'frigerator,' she told him, extending two small hands towards it.

'Well, it's *red* wine. You don't put it in the fridge.'

She frowned up at him. 'Are you s'posed to drink it hot?'

'Eh, not exactly. It's supposed to be served at room temperature.'

'So how do you know the temperature of the room?'

Craig blinked. 'Um, where's your mother?'

'Upstairs. Uncle Bernie hasn't come down yet so she's probably still getting dressed.'

Knowing Taylor had no living relatives and he had none called Bernie, the child's casual revelation that there was a man upstairs while Taylor was dressing did ugly things to Craig's blood pressure.

'*Who*,' he asked through clenched teeth, 'is Uncle Bernie?'

'My dog. He's *really*, *really big*, but don't worry,' she advised. 'He's friendly.'

The force of Craig's relieved sigh was such that he marvelled that it hadn't blown the tiny girl off her feet. Yet his original anxiety hadn't been caused by a fear of canines; a killer Rottweiler upstairs wouldn't have worried him as much as a flesh-and-blood man! He wasn't shocked by the strength of his possessiveness towards Taylor; many a night he'd tortured himself by imagining her in the arms of another man and felt pain and anger claw at his gut. Yet only now did it occur to him that in five years there may well have been more than *one*. Looking at Melanie, he fleetingly speculated whether she could provide him with an answer to the question foremost in his mind. Was *she* his only rival for Taylor's affections or was there another?

No! He *would not* stoop so low as to pump the kid about her mother's love life. It was a sleazy, under-handed thing to do. He tuned out the inner voice suggesting his pseudo-nobility only disguised his real reason for not quizzing Melanie—fear she might tell him things he didn't want to know!

'Hi, Craig, sorry I wasn't ready when you got here.'

He pivoted at the voice of the woman he'd been aching to see for five days. Now he *was* seeing her, the ache intensified rather than lessened. Her hair was seductively tousled as if someone in the throes of passion had run eager fingers through its soft, tawny length, but how those hands could have strayed from the tempting curves of her body, detailed by the short black stretch dress she wore was beyond Craig's comprehension. He swallowed hard, his eyes following the shapely lines of her naked legs down to the spike-heeled shoes on her feet.

'Dinner shouldn't be too much longer,' she informed him. 'Unfortunately I'm a little behind schedule, but I'm sure Melanie will keep you occupied until I'm ready to serve.'

Her glossy smile was smooth, but the quick flick of her tongue at the corner of her mouth was enough to tell Craig she wasn't as cool or collected as she pretended. Past experience also told him she was every bit as *hot* as she looked.

He grinned at her. 'Well, I'm not averse to pitching in and helping with dinner,' he offered. 'You used to find me pretty...*handy* in the kitchen.'

Taylor blushed, her traitorous mind immediately flashing back—*as he'd intended*—to the times in their marriage when the kitchen counter had been utilized for purposes other than cooking. She tried to produce a patronizing look. 'No thanks. These days I manage very well on my own.'

He raised an eyebrow. 'Effective, but not nearly as much fun.' Taylor gasped so hard she started to choke. 'At least let me fix the drinks,' he insisted.

Her eyes still watering, she spoke to her daughter. 'Melanie, show your father where the bar is, please.'

'Then can I take him upstairs and show him Uncle Bernie?'

Then you can take him to hell! she thought. 'Sure, honey, whatever you want.' Without so much as glancing at Craig, she turned and hurried to the kitchen.

Taylor crouched in front of the open refrigerator, a thousand different emotions exploding within her, but anger held centre stage. Anger at herself. Looking down at the dress she'd hastily changed into at Craig's arrival, she wanted to scream. Dammit to hell, she was supposed to be trying to establish a relationship between her daughter and Craig! Not *re*-establish her own! And he'd been amused by her obvious attempt at self-promotion. *Smugly* amused! What was worse was that she still found his cocky, self-assured attitude as arousing as she had as a teenager! When he'd suggested giving her a hand in the kitchen, she'd damn near *salivated*.

'You've still got great legs.'

At the masculine observation, she leaped from her position, which had pushed the tight-fitting dress to the top of her thighs.

'I'm trying to cook in here! What do you want?' she demanded, dumping the head of lettuce onto the bench so hard it bounced. Her spine tingled with awareness as his eyes slid over her.

'Is that a trick question, or do you want the truth?'

Trying to ignore him, despite the fact that her hormones were overdosing with interest at the blatant innuendo, Taylor gave her attention to unwrapping the steaks. But his nearness was creating havoc with her senses, making her efforts to triumph over the plastic wrap slow and awkward. After several minutes of trying to pretend he wasn't there, she gave up the charade.

'Is there some reason you're just standing there? You're supposed to be visiting with Mel—'

'I brought your drink,' he said, holding her glass aloft.

She blushed, feeling stupidly juvenile, and accepted the drink then retreated against the counter.

'You look good, Tay.' He raised his glass as if the words were a toast. '*Really* good.'

So do you, she thought, but knew better than to say so. Not because she was trying to score points off him, but because she didn't want to verbally acknowledge what her eyes, brain and hormones were beating her over the head with! That blue denim jeans looked better moulding *his* hard muscular thighs than those of any male model breathing; that the yoke of his shirt accentuated his broad shoulders, making her hands itch to caress them; and that his lips, closing over the rim of his glass, sent a million sparks of desire raining through her bloodstream.

At the sound of Melanie calling his name, Craig's mouth twisted in annoyance; his reaction was sufficient to snap Taylor back to reality.

'She's lots of things she wants to show you,' Taylor said. 'So you'd better go.'

Shaking his head, he reached out a hand to touch her hair. 'I'd much rather stay here with you.'

She pulled back. 'That's *not* the reason you're here.'

'Isn't it?'

'No, dammit, it's not!' she snapped, angry he could disregard Melanie's feelings so easily. She was about to tell him as much, but the child's appearance denied her the chance.

'Come see Uncle Bernie, Daddy,' she said, taking Craig's hand and tugging. 'Mummy gets cross if you talk to her when she's trying to cook.'

He left hand in hand with his daughter, but it seemed to Taylor he was back under her feet in no time. She was dishing dinner when she sensed she was no longer alone. Though his approach had been silent, she recognized the scent of his aftershave and the almost-physical touch of his gaze. She forced herself not to turn around.

'You remembered steak was one of my favourites, umm?'

'You were only getting stir fry, but I missed getting to the butcher's. Steak was all I had in the freezer. Don't flatter yourself that I'm trying to impress you.'

'You've never had to *try* to impress me, Tay. You do it just by breathing.'

His seductive tone laid a carpet of goose bumps over her, causing her hand to tremble. Worried she'd slice the top of her finger along with the celery, she dropped the knife, reached for her half-empty drink and finished it before turning to him. Yet the hope that a shot of alcohol would immunize her against the effect this man had on her was a futile one and the impact of his dark, brooding handsomeness was such that she had to steady herself against the Formica counter. The electricity arcing between them, even from a distance of two feet, would have electrocuted anyone attempting to pass between them. The notion immediately reminded Taylor that five years ago someone had.

'Where's Melanie?' she asked.

'Upstairs. Putting away her battalion of Barbie dolls, like I told her to.'

Taylor gave him a doubtful look. 'Yeah, right, and pigs mi...' Her words died as Melanie charged into the room looking enormously pleased with herself.

'Hey, Mummy, I put my things away all by myself,' she said.

Forcing a smile, Taylor muttered, 'Good girl,' to her daughter, despite resenting the fact Craig had apparently secured good-natured compliance in a few minutes for a task that required *her* to beg, plead and threaten in order to get results. Even pouting ones! She slanted a quick look at the man in question. *How dare he display better parenting skills than her*!

His grin was blatantly smug. '*You're* obviously too soft on her,' he commented, his mind-reading irritating her even more.

'Beginner's luck!' she snapped. 'Besides, "new toys" always get the most attention from a child, but eventually the *novelty* wears off, Craig.'

'*Touché.*'

The dullness of his response made her regret her bitchiness.

By the time Taylor had tucked her daughter into bed, she was an emotional mess! Her nerves were stretched tightrope taut, and knowing that even now Craig was watching her every move didn't help.

During dinner she hadn't been able to relax for one second. Not even Melanie's childish chatter could distract her from noticing the way Craig had been visually stripping her through the entire meal, optically devouring her with a relish suggesting he considered *her* dessert. What was worse was no matter how hard she'd tried, she couldn't stop recollections of the feast of pleasure they'd provided each other in the past from creeping into her mind and bringing with them a vaporous heat, which had curled its way through her body.

'Can't I *please* have a story, Mummy?'

'No, Mel, you've already stayed up for an extra hour. You've got school tomorrow.'

There were a few more beseeching pleas followed up by mutinous mutterings from the youngster, but Taylor remained firm, constantly conscious of the amused male eyes on her.

'Good night and God bless, sweetheart,' she said, bending to kiss her daughter. Little arms wrapped around her neck and Taylor gave thanks that God had decided to trust her with Melanie's life.

'Your turn, Daddy,' the child said, releasing her mother.

Taylor's heart turned over at her daughter's request and the eager pleasure shining in her young eyes. Had Melanie missed having a father to kiss her good-night? Had she found Taylor's mother love insufficient? The thought cut her to the quick.

Realizing Craig had made no move towards the child, she spun around, intending to *glare* him into compliance. Instead she found herself in his arms.

'Daddy's turn,' he whispered before the touch of his mouth immobilized her.

The gentleness of his tongue slipping over her bottom lip pushed Taylor's heart into overdrive; its pounding pace echoed in her ears and made her tremble. But all too quickly she was released and the pulsating drumming was replaced by childish giggles.

'No, silly!' Melanie chided. 'You're s'posed to kiss *me*!'

'Ah!' Craig said, drawing more giggles with his pseudo-innocent tone. '*Now* I get it!'

Shaken to the core, Taylor bolted from the room.

CHAPTER FIVE

IT WAS fifteen minutes before Craig joined her in the family room, and, though still rattled by his kiss, Taylor was determined not to show it. Setting aside her coffee cup, she began pouring one for him.

'You always did make the world's best coffee. I don't think I've had a decent cup since you left.'

She would have challenged the exaggeration if her mind—and body—hadn't become totally distracted by his presence beside her on the sofa. Alarmed, she sprang to her feet, the movement drawing a puzzled frown from Craig.

'What's wrong?' he asked.

'I...eh...I forgot the after-dinner mints.'

'Don't worry, I don't want any.'

'I do.'

She fled the room, calling herself a stupid fool only to return five minutes later feeling an even bigger one. Craig was fiddling with her elaborate sound system, and the laid-back lyrics of Jimmy Buffett were drifting softly in the air. A slow smile creased his face.

'Couldn't find the mints?'

She blushed, but tried to distract him from noticing by answering with a careless shrug. 'Forgot I was out of them. Eh, would you like another coffee?'

He shook his head; coffee was the furthest thing from his mind. What he wanted was *her*. He was weak with want for her—her touch, her passion, the taste of her femininity. He exhaled in a rush as his loins tightened in desire. Taylor was desire and femininity personified. *Perfection* personified.

He smiled, recalling how until he'd met her he'd classed himself as a 'legs man', but after one look at Taylor Radcliffe, his range of appreciation immediately expanded. Sure, her long, smooth legs had been second to none, but so was the rest of her; her bottom and hips were in perfectly proportioned contrast to her tiny waist and high, firm breasts, and the elegant line of her neck and patrician facial features stunning in their own right. The waist-length honey blond hair he remembered might be gone and there was a new air of maturity about her, but those changes counted for nothing. Taylor still bore the sleek, flowing gracefulness God had gift-wrapped her in and she was still the most desirable woman Craig had ever known.

Uncomfortable under the intensity of his gaze, Taylor self-consciously smoothed her hands over her hips before a flare of desire in Craig's eyes told her he'd interpreted the action as provocative. Her stomach fluttered at the thought, making her wonder half-guiltily if, regardless of her best intentions, her subconscious had *intended* him to misinterpret the nervous gesture. If so, she was in trouble. Big trouble.

With Mel in bed, she could no longer count on the child to act as a release valve for the sensual tension that had been building up all night. She and Craig were on their own now, and, given their past track record for succumbing to lust over level-headedness, things didn't bode well. Taking a deep breath, she fought to gain control of the situation. Deciding that returning to the sofa was tempting fate, she quickly moved to the farthest armchair and sat down.

'You're staring, Craig.'

He took two steps toward her. 'I can't help it.' Two more long-legged strides brought him closer still. 'You're beautiful.'

'I...' A strange blend of excitement, fear and desire strangled whatever response she'd been going to make and began permeating her body as he continued to shorten the distance between them. By the time he stopped, only inches from her, Taylor's heart was pounding as if it would explode. As she looked up into his eyes, a vague dizziness swept over her. Though perhaps it had nothing to do with his eyes and everything to do with the way he clasped her hands and tugged her to her feet.

'I realize we need to talk, Tay...' His words brushed her cheek. 'But I need to do this more.'

She could no more have stopped her arms from wrapping around his solid male frame than she could have stepped away from his kiss. In a distant region of her brain, she registered that finally having contact with his body relieved her from the crushing emotional pressure she'd been experiencing for days, but hadn't understood what was causing it. Now she knew— curiosity.

Curiosity as to whether her memories of Craig's love-making mastery were accurate or if her mind had merely embroidered them as a means of justifying her once-wanton reaction to them. When his tongue plunged inside her mouth, Taylor had her answer.

To feel a part of him moving within her after all these years threw her senses into chaos, intensifying them to the point where she could actually *feel* and *hear* her blood circulating through her body; could *smell* the desire seeping from their pores and could almost *taste* hot male arousal. She rose to her toes, desperate to get closer to the solid, hard maleness of him, her hands moving with desperate urgency across his shoulders and back. For five years she had dreamed of this man. *Ached* for this man. Now she could again experience him....

Craig had never known such an overwhelming sense of gratefulness as he did when Taylor's arms closed around him. He devoured her mouth, driven by the need to have the heat of her passion defrost his too-long frozen soul. His life had been so empty without this woman. More like an existence than a life! The taste of her after half a decade was the most exhilarating thing he'd ever experienced, the warmth of her body the most sensual. He cupped her breast, and her low purr of approval made him almost as mindless as the touch of her lips at his throat.

'Oh, Tay! I've missed you so much! I've almost died from wanting you,' he muttered, burying his face in her hair, only to again return to the nectar sweetness of her mouth as desire hummed through his blood. The flavour and feel of her made him feel weak and powerful at the same time. He couldn't get enough of her.

'Tay, honey,' he rasped, 'I've been crazy without you. Let's go upstairs...'

Dazed by desire, he took several seconds to realize that the warm, responsive woman in his arms had suddenly become rigid and was struggling to withdraw from his embrace. Opening his eyes, he was shocked to see tears slipping silently down her cheeks. In momentary confusion, he relaxed his embrace, allowing her the opportunity to move away. She eluded his attempt to recapture her.

'Tay... honey?'

'This is where the night ends, Craig.'

He swore, moving to catch hold of her hand as she tried to turn away. 'What the hell do you mean, *this is where the night ends*?'

'I mean,' she said, trying to tug her wrist from his grasp, 'I want you to go home. *Now*.'

'Liar,' he said, feeling the speed of her pulse as rapid and eager as his own. 'Your body gives you away, babe. It always has.'

A flash of anger sparked in her green eyes. 'So?' she challenged. 'These days, I listen to my brain, not my libido! *I* take into account how my actions might hurt other people—'

'Believe me, honey, send me home now—' he glanced pointedly at the bulge in his jeans '—and we'll both ache all night.'

Taylor felt her insides cramp with desire as memories from the past raced through her mind. The urge to give in to him was almost overwhelming and it took more will-power than she credited herself with possessing to shake her head. What happened tonight would involve someone other than the two of them; it would involve Melanie. Freeing herself from his grasp, she told him as much.

'Craig, our wants aren't the only ones we have to consider. What about Melanie?'

'She's asleep! Don't tell me you need a five-year-old's permission to make love to a man *you're still married to*!'

In that instant, Taylor hated him. 'Damn you!' she cried. 'Could you just *pretend* to like her?'

'I do like her.'

'No, you don't! You simply see her as a means to get to *me*. You wangled this dinner by manipulating Melanie, and you know it!'

'OK, I admit that wasn't being completely up front, but—'

'There's no excuse, Craig. Melanie is just a little girl. I won't have her hurt.'

Surprisingly, her inference that he'd deliberately harm the child stung. 'Let's get one thing straight right now!' he commanded. 'Even though I never wanted children, I'd no more deliberately hurt that kid than I would you!'

'But you *did* hurt me, Craig. Pain can exist even without intent.' The damage of her own words immediately registered in his face, but she felt no pride in the fact and quickly lowered her gaze.

'You left *me*, Taylor, not the other way round. So don't talk to me about hurt. I loved you. I still do.'

The words came out as if he didn't have the strength to hold them in. She stepped back, shaking her head.

'It's the truth, Tay. In spite of everything that happened—'

'You mean in spite of the fact I conceived Melanie against your wishes?' she challenged, wondering if he would ever understand that without trust declarations of love meant nothing. 'Or in spite of the fact she *exists*? What about her, Craig? What exactly do you feel for Melanie?'

'Jeez, Taylor!' He ran an aggrieved hand through his hair. 'She's only been in my life five minutes! How can I be sure *what* I feel? I barely know her!'

'Since you've no one to blame for her absence from your life other than yourself—'

'You took her with you!' he accused. 'You couldn't even wait until I was in the country to tell me face to face!'

'I did what was best for Melanie! She needed to be surrounded by love not—'

'Yeah, right. And she's had your love for as long as I haven't.'

'That's a stupid comment! Parental love isn't the same as . . . as what we had.'

'So tell me, which is stronger, Taylor?' he asked. 'Because I know from firsthand experience they can't coexist.'

She knew he was referring to the fact that his parents, who'd been happily married and childless for eighteen years before he was born, had divorced within two years of his birth. Neither had ever had any qualms about telling Craig that they each held him responsible for the failure of the marriage.

Taylor had no intention of ever letting that kind of guilt fall onto Melanie. Nor did she believe Craig would ever be so cruel. Still, she had no words with which to answer his question as to which love was stronger. All she could offer in response was a helpless shrug and a shake of her head. He sighed heavily as if he'd pinned all his hopes on her being able to tell him.

'Look,' he said, shoving his hands into his pockets, 'I admit I haven't been any sort of father to Melanie in the past, and lord knows my background doesn't provide me with many examples of what a father should and shouldn't do, but... I'd like to try to be one now.' He raised hopeful eyes to her. 'If you'll let me.'

Taylor turned away, choked with emotion. Almost a full minute passed before she could speak and even then her voice was unsteady. 'All right, Craig... you can see her.'

She watched his shoulders sag as if he'd been holding his breath for her answer. 'Thank you. I appreciate the second chance even if I don't deserve it.'

Nodding, she began clearing away the coffee things.

'Would it be OK if I came over on Friday to see her?' he asked. 'Unfortunately I have a meeting in Canberra tomorrow and I won't be back until late, but I'm free Friday night. We could go to the movies.'

She couldn't help smiling at his obvious eagerness. Clearly he wasn't going to waste any time.

'I don't see why not. But you'd have to pick her up before six o'clock,' she told him, carrying the coffee tray to the kitchen. 'I have basketball.'

'I meant all of us could go. You know a... a *family* outing.'

Taylor's blood froze and only a miracle allowed her to deposit the tray on the bench before it fell from her hands. The image of Craig, Melanie and herself as a typical family was out of focus, fuzzy and blurred like a badly tuned television screen. Of course, you could adjust a television and fine-tune it, but Taylor wasn't convinced the same could be done with relationships. Especially one like theirs, where the emotional wiring was in such a tangle.

'I don't think that's a good idea, Craig. You and Melanie need time to yourselves.'

'Dammit, Taylor! What about what *we* need?'

'I'm not sure I know what we need, Craig,' she said, amazing herself with her calmness. 'But right now, it's Melanie I'm concerned about. I want her to get to know you and I don't want emotional baggage from our past complicating things.'

Craig shook his head, a bemused look on his face. 'OK, Tay, we'll play by your rules. But it's not the past that worries you. It's the future.'

CHAPTER SIX

ON FRIDAY after returning Melanie's excited wave as she drove away in Craig's Porsche, Taylor remained in the doorway for several moments after the car had disappeared, trying to come to terms with the mixed emotions she felt.

She could have gone. Craig had again tried to convince her to opt out of the basketball game, but she'd refused. In her heart she knew it was best for Melanie that she have her father to herself; she'd waited *so* long for the chance. Yet Taylor was honest enough to acknowledge her good intentions were somewhat frayed at the edges; a part of her couldn't be noble about seeing the unrestrained delight that had lit Melanie's face as she'd scampered into the low-level sports car, thrilled at being with her father.

'Get a grip, Taylor,' she told herself. 'A trip to the movies doesn't equate with a custody battle.'

As soon as she said the words, Taylor felt ill.

Three hours later, she gave a grateful sigh as her coach indicated he was making a substitution. Slumping onto the bench, she reached into her sports bag and rummaged about until she felt the coldness of her drink bottle. Pulling it out, she took a long swallow of the refreshingly cool glucose mixture.

'What's the score?'

Gagging on the drink, she jerked around to find the voice's owner crouching behind her.

'Craig! What are you doing here? Where's—?'

'Hi, Mummy! Are you winning?'

Taylor nodded, indicating the electric scoreboard. 'Wh-what are the pair of you doing here?' she repeated.

'Daddy said it would be a good idea if we picked you up before we went to McDonald's! Then we could *all* have burgers!'

Melanie's tone implied she thought the idea was full of merit. Taylor didn't.

'We phoned your place and didn't get an answer, so we took a punt and came here from the movie.' Craig lowered his mouth to her ear. 'I'd forgotten how sexy you looked in a sweat-soaked singlet.'

Craig's slow appraisal of her body as she stood up didn't do anything to improve her respiration rate. If anything, she was even more breathless now than when she'd first left the court.

'Taylor! You're on for Gina!'

'Ummm, I have to go. I . . . we're nearly finished.' She hated that she was stammering like a schoolgirl.

'Hey, Adams!' the team's grandfatherly coach bellowed. 'You here to play or chit-chat? On the court!'

Trying to ignore the amused look Craig sent her, Taylor threw herself into the game with renewed gusto, but her concentration wasn't what it should have been and she tripped over the feet of one of her own players and went crashing to the floor. The hard surface rattled her bones, but with the game continuing around her, she instinctively tried to spring back to her feet. She failed; scorching pain knifed her in the knee.

Grasping her leg with both hands, she tried unsuccessfully to bite down on the anguished cry that tore at her throat. She screwed her face up in an effort to stop the pain, a pain so intense even closed eyes couldn't prevent tears from rolling down her cheeks. Team-mates began crowding around her, but with her senses blurred by agony, she couldn't identify who was saying what.

'You okay?'

'What happened?'

'Think she rolled her ankle...'

Finally someone got it right. 'Is it your knee?'

She nodded, then immediately shook her head as someone tried to pry her hands away from the injured area.

'Oh, God!' she cried, tossing her head in an effort to shake free of the fire burning up her leg. 'It hurts like all hell!'

As she said the words, she felt herself being swept up in a pair of strong, familiar arms. Of its own accord, her head lowered against a firm, muscular chest.

'Take it easy, sweetheart,' Craig murmured softly.

'Easy for... you to say,' she said, grimacing. 'It's not your leg that's falling off.' A sudden thought struck her. 'It's... it's not broken, is it?' Craig's averted eyes and the straight, tight line of his mouth were her only response.

With infinite care, he lowered her onto the court side bench. Again someone shoved a drink towards her, and again she shook her head. It was going to take more than a swig of Gatorade to make her feel better!

'Mummy, are you okay?'

She'd forgotten Mel was here and hearing the worried tone in her daughter's voice made her forgetfulness seem that much worse.

'I've been better, sweethea— Aaahhh!' Taylor screamed as the pain suddenly increased.

'It's only an ice pack. Want to minimize the swelling.' The coach's tone was gruff but concerned. 'I want you to tell me where it hurts.'

Taylor gripped harder on the male hand intertwined with hers as the coach's probing touch moved up her calf, but when he finally pressed the outside region of her injured knee, her entire body lurched and she had to fight to bite back an obscenity.

'Sorry, kiddo.' The coach offered a weak smile. 'I'm being as gentle as I can.'

'Promise me you won't get rough!' she returned through clenched teeth. Turning her head, she caught sight of the white-knuckled grip she held on Craig's hand and attempted to withdraw her own, but he placed his other over it.

'No,' he said, trapping her grip. 'Concentrate on squeezing as tightly as you can. It'll keep your mind off the pain.'

It was well-intentioned advice she was sure! But if she'd had the strength to talk, Taylor could have told him it didn't have a snowball's chance in hell of working! Already it felt as if the pain had travelled to every part of her body and the dizzy sensation she was experiencing suggested her brain was being affected, too. Closing her eyes, she let her head drift back against a very solid, but very comfortable male shoulder.

Sensing Taylor was close to passing out, Craig glared at the grey-haired coach. 'Do you actually know what you're doing? Or are you simply determined to torture her?'

The remark earned him a look, half condescending, half martyred. 'Since I figure you're either her husband or her boyfriend, I'll ignore your tone, *son*. As for knowing what I'm doing, I've been in this game longer than you've been in long pants, so I'll back diagnosis of a busted kneecap even before I see an X-ray.'

Craig swore, hearing his worst fears confirmed, but judging by the way Taylor's face was contorting in pain, he doubted she was aware of anything being said.

'You right to get her to hospital on your own?' the old man asked, genuine concern showing in his face as he looked at Taylor's almost unconscious form.

'Yeah, I've got my car outside—' Craig stopped and cursed again. There was no way he'd be able to get her comfortable in the Porsche. He'd have to use her car. 'I'll need her car.' He spoke aloud and to no one in particular as he rose to his feet, trying not to jolt the woman in his arms. 'Someone fish her keys out of her bag for me.'

It was the coach who obliged. 'I'll drop the rest of her gear at her place later. Want someone to drop your car off there, too?'

Craig nodded. 'Thanks. The keys are in my pocket.' He angled himself so the man could get them. Becoming more and more concerned with Taylor's pallor, he turned and started towards the exit.

'Hey, mate!' the coach called. 'What about the kid?'

'What kid?' As soon as he asked the question, his eyes lit on an ashen-faced Melanie. *Damn*. The last thing Taylor needed was her chattering daughter firing questions at her when she was in pain.

The thought must have shown in his face because the old man said, 'Listen, if it'll be easier, I could keep her with me and drop her off—'

'No!' Melanie protested in a loud voice. 'I want to go with Mummy!'

Craig had to remind himself it was worry about her mother and not wilfulness that had the kid's mouth set so mutinously, but either way he didn't want to have to deal with a tantrum now.

'Look, Mel,' he said as reasonably as he could, 'it'll be better if you go with...with...'

Realizing that he didn't know a thing about the man he'd been about to foist his daughter on caused a sensation of sick guilt to fill his gut. Good one, Adams! he chided himself. You're about as qualified for responsible parenting as you are for brain surgery!

'Er, thanks,' he said, directing a grimace of a smile at the man. 'But I'd better take her with us.'

Through the haze of pain clouding her senses, Taylor was dimly aware of Craig lowering her into a wheelchair, then she was forced to close her eyes against the glare of the fluorescent lights. Strangely, the darkness did little to ease the throbbing in her leg and the wheel-chair felt cold compared to Craig's body.

'Jeez, Taylor, I thought you were smarter than to let this guy knock you off your feet again.'

The sound of a familiar female voice prompted her to once again open her eyes and try to focus. *Liz*! Pleased to discover her friend was working the night shift in Casualty, Taylor tried to smile.

Craig watched Taylor grimace, her greeting to Liz little more than a breathless mutter. The pallor of her face worried him and he roughly demanded she be given something to stop the pain. They were in a hospital, for God's sake!

'As soon as she's had the X-rays,' Liz told him, then turned to a young male nurse. 'Wheel Ms Adams down to radiology and tell them I want the results immediately. I'll be in night sister's office.'

'Yes, Dr O'Shea.'

As the nurse took hold of Taylor's wheelchair, Craig brushed his hands aside. 'I'll do it.'

'Sir, you can't! Hospital policy states—'

'Listen, don't start stating hospital policy to me! I said, *I'd* take her.'

'Craig,' Liz O'Shea intervened, 'why not take Mel down and get her a drink or something? There's nothing you can do at the moment.'

'Forget it, Liz. I'm staying with Taylor.'

'Me, too!' piped up Melanie. 'I'm going with Mummy.'

'Mel, you *can't*,' Liz said gently. 'Mummy has to be X-rayed.'

'Then I'm staying with Daddy!'

Craig swore. 'Melanie, be reasonable—'

Liz rolled her eyes. 'Oh, for heaven's sake, Craig! Five-year-olds don't know the meaning of the word *reasonable*. Besides, Mel is Taylor's and your daughter so she's probably genetically allergic to *reason*.'

The young nurse's face twitched at the remark and Craig would cheerfully have knocked him into the middle of next week had it not been for the fact Taylor reached for his hand.

'I'll be okay... truly. Just look after Mel. Please?'

He withstood her pleading green eyes for all of three seconds. Sighing, he ran a hand around the back of his neck, then nodded. But the uncertainty he felt about leaving Taylor must have shown even as he took hold of the little girl's hand.

'Hey, don't look so worried,' Liz told him. 'The kid doesn't bite. At least not any more.'

Huh! thought Craig. How could she? She talked so much her teeth were never together! He knew because she'd been chattering non-stop since he'd picked her up for the movies. Yet it occurred to him now that Melanie had been almost totally silent since her mother's fall. Turning to the child, he saw the tell-tale tremble of her bottom lip as Taylor was wheeled away and he was assailed by a wave of sympathy. Crouching down to her level, he produced what he hoped was a convincing smile.

'Hey,' he said, 'how about we go find ourselves a Coke?'

Doubtful brown eyes darted from his face to the corridor Taylor had disappeared down. 'Is... is Mummy going to be all right?'

'Oh, sure she is, kiddo! Mummy's going to be fine.'

The force of the tiny body launching itself at him threw him off balance in more ways than one.

By the time she was wheeled back to the examination cubicle, Taylor was convinced she was in worse shape than when she'd arrived! The hulk-size radiologist had been about as gentle as a sledgehammer!

The nurse left, saying he would notify Dr O'Shea that the X-rays were complete, and alone in the typical-looking clinical room, Taylor considered the implications of her injury.

She'd probably be off her leg for at least a week, which meant she'd have to revise her intentions not to have a full-time housekeeper. Financially there was no reason she hadn't employed a housekeeper since arriving in Sydney. It was just that she enjoyed having the house to Melanie and herself, and had planned only to hire someone part-time even when she started work—

'What's the verdict?'

Craig's voice startled her from her thoughts. 'I...I don't know yet. I'm waiting for Liz to come back.' Her eyes went to Melanie's limp form cradled in his arms. 'Is she asleep?'

'Either that or she talked herself to death,' he said, placing the child on one of the room's two examination tables. 'I'll have Liz check her pulse when she gets here.'

Taylor tried to smile, but a twinge of pain turned it into a grimace. Instantly, Craig was next to her, crouching beside the wheelchair and slipping a lock of stray hair from her face. This time, her sudden intake of breath wasn't caused by her injury, but by hot splinters of excitement flickering down her spine as his fingers moved to caress her cheek and jaw.

'Did they give you anything to stop the pain?'

She nodded. 'But it's not kicking in yet.'

His nearness was causing the most erratic sensations to occur in her chest, and if she'd been having her heart monitored, the machines would be going haywire! Filled with a sudden desire to run her tongue along the two-inch scar he sported below his left eye, she clamped her teeth together—a precaution should the temptation override her common sense. An unconscious movement caused her knee to protest, a groan escaping even through her still-clenched teeth.

'You know,' Craig said, stroking her bare thigh with one finger, 'I know a terrific way of making you forget your injury—'

'I'm sure you do,' Liz said from the doorway. 'But it might prove difficult with Taylor in plaster!'

'*Plaster*!' Taylor wailed. 'You mean ...'

'You, my dear girl, have a hairline fracture of the patella. Or in layman's terms, a broken kneecap.'

'Oh, no, Liz! I don't believe this!' She sent Liz a look that begged her to say she was joking. She didn't. 'Great!' she muttered. 'Just terrific! *Plaster*! For how long?'

'Four, maybe five weeks. It depends entirely on how quickly it heals,' Liz told her.

'*What*?' Taylor couldn't believe what she was hearing. 'How am I going to function? I mean, I have to drive Melanie to school. I was supposed to go check out two job possibilities on Monday. What am I supposed to do for the next month?'

'As little as possible, I'd say!' Craig teased while pondering her comment that she had to check out job possibilities.

Even without her income from Adams Relief, Taylor was one of the wealthiest women in the country. Her father, Sir Douglas Radcliffe, had been one of Australia's most respected business barons, and on his death, Taylor had inherited sole control of two mining conglomerates, a national transport company and the largest chain of jewellery stores in Australia. His thoughts were drowned out by Taylor's continuing to voice disbelief at her friend's diagnosis.

'Liz, are you sure they haven't misread the X-ray? I mean, I've *never* broken anything in my life! I *can't* have a broken leg!'

'Kneecap,' the redhead corrected. 'And there's a first time for everything! So accept it, OK? It could be worse.'

'Yeah, right,' Taylor muttered.

'Cheer up,' Liz said. 'Good thing you did this tonight and not tomorrow, because I'd have been flying to that conference in Cairns. And since we aren't busy tonight, I'll personally apply the cast.'

Taylor gave a false smile. 'Yippee.'

'This one is only temporary, though,' her friend went on, opening cupboards and extracting a variety of dishes and packages. 'I've called in a favour I'm owed and arranged for an orthopaedic specialist to have a look at you first thing tomorrow. After that, you can get a fibreglass job done if you like.'

Taylor was feeling too sorry for herself to care whether they set the leg in concrete or solid gold. *Four weeks*! Lord, what was she going to do? She looked across at her sleeping daughter, and her predicament seemed even worse. How would she cope with Mel like this?

The concept of coping made her wonder how Melanie had enjoyed her outing with Craig. Better than he did, she'd say if the grim expression on his face now was any indication. And judging by the time they'd turned up at the stadium, he'd not spared any time in getting to and from the movie! Nor did his earlier comments about Mel's talking make it sound as if he was exactly chafing at the bit for another dose of paternal recreation. It didn't surprise her, so why should it upset her?

'There's really no need for you to stay,' she told him. 'It's nearly midnight.'

Craig wasn't immune to the cool tone she used, nor was he in the mood to try to tease her out of it. He *knew* the time and he was damned tired! He'd been a mass of nerves waiting for tonight to arrive and not a bloody thing had gone the way he'd anticipated! He hadn't been able to talk Taylor into coming out with them, and when he'd turned up at the basketball court ready to activate plan B, she'd sabotaged that, as well, by injuring her knee. If he wasn't an intelligent, reasonable, thirty-two-year-old, he'd have believed she'd done it deliberately!

'Planning on jogging home, are you?' he asked.

'I can take a taxi.'

'Somehow I can't see a cab driver carrying you *and* a sleeping Melanie into the house and upstairs.'

'I'm sure the hospital issues crutches along with leg casts.' Craig gave her a hard look of impatience. 'Look, Craig, I appreciate your help—'

'Good! But it's not finished yet so save the gratuitous speech until I've got you home and into bed.'

He hadn't intended the remark to be suggestive. But it was and the tension that engulfed the room proved they were both remembering other times when such speeches had consisted of passion-inspired nonsensical mutterings. He looked up to discover Liz O'Shea watching them with studious interest. When she pinned him with a narrow gaze, he sensed she wanted to say something but was holding herself in check. She went back to applying the cast, and with a muttered announcement that he needed some air, he left them.

Liz was Taylor's oldest and dearest friend and Craig had met her the night he'd met Taylor; but whereas it had been love at first sight between him and Taylor, it had been hard, suspicious glares at twenty paces as far as he and Liz were concerned. By unspoken agreement he and the redhead had, for Taylor's sake, tolerated each other while he and Tay had been married, but until tonight Craig hadn't seen Liz O'Shea since the day his marriage had ended. But he'd sensed her disapproval at his re-emergence in Taylor's life.

Just outside the glassed entrance of Casualty, Craig propped himself against the wall and drew a series of deep breaths. Reflecting how in just one week his past had become the present and wondering what the future held.

* * *

It had to have been more than an hour later, when, responding to the sound of his name, Craig turned to find Liz O'Shea at the entrance of the hospital.

'Finished?' he asked. At the woman's nod, he moved towards the double glass doors. 'Right then, I'll take her home.'

'Wait!'

'What's up?' He tensed, noting the concern on Liz's face.

'You tell me,' she returned.

'I'm not in the mood for games—'

'Neither is Taylor,' Liz said, cutting him short.

'Meaning?'

'Meaning only an idiot could miss the electricity that still exists between you and Taylor, and I pride myself on being a long way smarter than that. On your good days I think even you might be!'

'Get to the point, Liz.'

'The point *is* that no matter how you feel about Taylor, it isn't worth a damn unless you remember that she comes as a package deal now. And the package reads Fragile—Handle With Care!'

He made no response; he didn't have to. They both knew her words were the truth. While he and Liz had never been friends, he knew the redhead's friendship for Taylor couldn't be questioned. It seemed her staunch affection now extended to Melanie.

Melanie. The package deal. The child who had been only nine inches long when she was born. Looking down at his ten-and-a-half-inch hand span, he tried to visualize the little girl reduced to that size. It was beyond him. Just as so much about the child was beyond him. How could anyone put up with the inane chatter and endless questions she seemed to fire out non-stop? He'd never met anyone who could change subjects thirty times before drawing a breath!

She was stubborn, too, he suspected, recalling the mutinous set of her mouth when he'd considered leaving her with the old basketball coach. Of course, she'd get that from her mother! he thought with affectionate amusement. Taylor was the most stubborn woman he had ever met. And the most beautiful. She was also the only woman he would ever love. Having lived without her for five years, he didn't want to ever do it again. The trouble was, he didn't think he was ready for a package deal. Nor it seemed did Liz O'Shea. But he wasn't about to share his doubts.

'Anything else you want to get off your chest, Liz? Because if not, I'll go take Taylor home.'

'Actually there is,' she informed him. 'This goes against my better judgement, but I suggest you stay the night at Taylor's.'

'You *what*?'

'Close your mouth, Craig,' she said drily. 'I said *stay* at Taylor's, not *sleep* with her. The cast isn't completely dry and if Mel wants anything during the night, Taylor won't be able to manage the crutches. If I wasn't on duty I'd do it, but...' She shrugged.

When Craig remained silent, she said, 'Look, if it's a prob—'

'It's not a problem, Liz.' He shook his head, not bothering to conceal his amusement. 'You know, I never imagined *you* in the role of *my* fairy godmother.'

'Believe me, Craig, if I was in the position to grant wishes, Taylor would have two good legs and *you'd* be croaking on a lily-pad!'

CHAPTER SEVEN

SUBCONSCIOUSLY sensing the safe cocoon of slumber beginning to unravel around her, Taylor buried her head in a pillow to muffle the intrusion of a male voice debating with an excited child's.

'Quiet down! You'll wake her up.'

'But I *always* wake her at this time.'

'Not *this* morning you don't. She'll be tired.'

'Nah, she won't.'

Sleepily she prayed that both the ache in her leg and the intrusive dream would recede and allow her some peace, but she lost all confidence in the power of prayer when the door of her bedroom burst open amid squeals of childish delight.

'Look, Mummy! *Daddy's still here.*'

The announcement made Taylor's eyes fly open and her heart skip. The vital organ stopped completely when her bleary gaze encountered a piercing brown male one over the head of her daughter.

'He *slept* here, Mummy. *All night*!'

The word that slipped from Taylor's lips sprang as much from the sight of Craig Adams standing in the doorway of her bedroom, as from the pain of her encased right leg slamming into her left ankle as Melanie leaped onto the bed.

'Don't worry, Daddy,' the little girl said, sending a reassuring smile to the jeans-clad man. 'Mummy's always a bit grumpy before she has her coffee.'

'Yeah,' he drawled, 'I know.' The heated brown-eyed glance he directed at her did worrying things to her heart rate even before he gave a lazy smile. ''Course I also know of other things that have been proven to improve her mood,' he added.

'Like what?' the little girl wanted to know.

'Nothing, Mel,' Taylor said quickly, giving Craig her most quelling look and trying to tell herself her body wasn't responding to the blatantly masculine appraisal he was giving her. But even without looking down at the direction of his gaze, she knew her breasts were reacting to it and that the thinness of her nightgown advertised as much.

She reefed the sheet up from her waist to her chin and tried to keep it there as she made an effort to sit up. Lying flat on her back while this man visually devoured her was inviting her hormones to riot.

Craig watched her awkward struggle, not trusting himself to assist her. This close, the sight of her, in gold satin, sleep-tousled and slightly disorientated, brought back too many memories that fired his blood. He shifted his position to lean against the door jamb, crossing one leg over the other in the hope his stance would be interpreted as nonchalance. Unlike Taylor, he had no sheet to shield his body's response.

In the hour since Melanie had woken and discovered his presence on the downstairs sofa, she'd been chattering non-stop, so it came as no surprise to him that she was the one to break the silence hanging in the room.

'Oh, wow!' she exclaimed, scampering from the bed. 'Stilts! Can I have a go?'

'They're crutches not stilts,' Taylor corrected. 'And *no*, you can't have a go. They're too big and you'll only hurt yourself playing with them.'

He watched silently as Melanie employed a series of assurances, ploys and pleas to get her mother to reverse the decision. The kid was a tenacious little thing, he'd give her that, but he sensed Taylor wasn't as determined to have the final word as she might have been in his absence. In fact, he'd bet the Porsche she was hoping to continue the verbal tennis match until he lost interest in the proceedings and boredom sent him retreating downstairs. Well, he'd lost interest long ago, but he'd have to be five years dead to be bored in the presence of this woman. His gut tightened. Compared to how he'd felt since she'd entered his office last week, he *had* been dead for the past five years.

'Melanie,' he said, forcefully interrupting the volley of dialogue, 'if you really want to try a pair of crutches, I'll hire you a pair from a chemist shop, OK?'

The child's cheer was loud, but Taylor's green-eyed glare was practically thunderous. It screamed that she considered his comment intrusive and indulgent.

'She has to learn she can't do or have everything she wants, Craig.'

'*Don't we all*?'

She was uncertain if his remark was intended as res-ignation or sarcasm, and before she could decide, he was speaking again.

'So tell me, how's the leg feel this morning?'

'Exactly how you'd expect it to feel,' she responded. 'It aches like the devil and weighs a ton.' His gaze went straight to her night stand and Taylor was glad she'd left the photo she kept of him in the drawer where she'd shoved it the night he'd come to dinner.

'You should've taken those painkillers Liz gave you.'

'I would have, if I'd been capable of swallowing the damn things.' She held one of the huge tablets between her fingers so he could see it.

'If you'd said something, I would have crushed them for you.'

'I was hardly going to wake you at three in the morning.'

'Assuming I was asleep,' he said.

'Only someone in intense pain *wouldn't* be asleep at that hour.'

Agitation bracketed his mouth. 'True. But then not all pain is physical.'

The suggestion that memories from their past had kept him sleepless jolted Taylor. For the first time, she acknowledged that, like her, Craig would be confronting their past—but from his own perspective. No doubt his view of the bad times would be completely different from hers, but knowing the good would be as seductively disturbing as her own was something she didn't want to think about. To do so was too arousing to *her* desires, especially when what could satisfy them stood only metres away....

Bad thought! Fiercely she shoved the notion aside. *She would not let her libido complicate her life any more than it already had*! Their history showed that physical satisfaction wasn't the be-all and end-all of what she needed in a relationship. *Trust* was what counted in the end. And Taylor knew she couldn't count on Craig's.

'You know, Mel,' she heard him say, 'you're right in what you say about your mother being moody until she gets her morning coffee into her. And judging by that scowl she's wearing, and since I doubt she'll agree to any alternatives I might suggest, I'd say this is a day for copious cups of caffeine.'

The child frowned. 'Does that mean a lot?'

He nodded. 'Now all we need to decide is if I should carry it up to her *or* . . . carry her down to it.'

Unlike her daughter, Taylor didn't find the latter suggestion the least bit amusing.

'Neither! I'm quite capable of going downstairs for breakfast under my own steam.'

Craig shook his head. 'I'm not sure that's a good idea—'

'*I* am,' she said. 'Now I'd appreciate if it you'd get out so I can shower and dress.'

His smirk was pure sin. 'I'm sure you'd *appreciate* it more if I stuck around and lent you a hand doing that...you being in plaster and all.'

She considered launching a pillow at his head, but dismissed the idea on the grounds it wouldn't inflict sufficient damage.

'As you said, I'm in plaster. Believe me, I'd have to be brain-dead, Craig Adams, before I'd take you up on *that* offer. So *go*!'

Even after she managed to get out of bed and undergo an awkward and unsatisfying shower, it still took Taylor twenty minutes to dress and another ten just to get down the stairs. Craig and Melanie were eating by the time she hobbled towards the table. While both turned and watched the last few metres of her approach, it was Craig's attention that unnerved her the most.

Oh, great! The last thing she needed was *his* handsome face turning the only fully functional knee she had left weak at the sight of him!

Conscious of two pairs of dark brown eyes studying her progress, Taylor moved with a painstaking care that only served to highlight her clumsiness. She all but collapsed into the chair Craig pulled back for her.

Melanie cheered and clapped. 'Yea! You made it!' Then her face broke into a huge peanut-butter grin. 'You look funny, Mummy! Can I bring some friends over to see you?'

The little girl was immune to the less-than-maternal glare the comment earned her. 'Gee, Mel, why don't you just drag me into school for show and tell?'

'We don't do show and tell yet,' the child replied seriously.

'Thank God for that,' Taylor muttered, picking up her knife and fork with the intention of digging into what looked like a very appealing stack of pancakes.

'You should have accepted my offer to help you down the stairs,' Craig said, reaching past her to whisk the plate of food from in front of her. 'I put this out when I saw you at the top of the stairs, but you took so long getting here it'll have to go into the microwave and be reheated.'

Grunting, she snatched the plate back. 'They'll be fine as they are.' Then, realizing she was hardly being gracious considering that he'd not only cooked breakfast, but also spent hours at the hospital, she forced a smile and tried to atone.

'I'm sorry. I should be thanking you for this,' she said, motioning to her plate. 'And for helping out last night. I do appreciate it. Really. It's just that if I'm to be incapacitated for a month, I'd best start getting the hang of it.'

'You better move into the downstairs bedroom or you'll break your neck getting the hang of it,' he said.

'I'll manage. Besides, I don't like sleeping too far away from Mel.'

He shrugged her remark aside. 'You haven't forgotten you've got an appointment with a specialist this morning, have you?'

Her fork stopping midway to her mouth, Taylor groaned. She'd been so groggy from the painkillers they'd fed her at the hospital, she was hard-pressed to recall anything that had happened after Liz had plastered her leg. She vaguely recalled her friend saying something about seeing a specialist. Damn, she didn't feel up to making her public début on crutches yet and said as much.

'You should be grateful Liz has the connections to wangle you an appointment in less than a few hours, let alone on a Saturday morning,' Craig told her, filling her coffee cup. 'I understand it can take months to get in to see an orthopaedic specialist.'

What he said was true, but right now she was finding it hard to feel grateful about *anything*. It was taking a chunk of will-power not to feel sorry for herself and all her mental power to block out the ocean of memories that facing Craig over breakfast activated. The thing she wanted most to do was the one thing her injury prevented her from doing—*running away as far and as fast as she could*!

After pouring himself coffee, Craig sat back in his chair, tuning out the rambunctious antics of Melanie and the huge dog she was feeding from her own plate, and studied the woman opposite him. Again he found himself marvelling at the sheer perfection of her make-up-free face and the changes he saw there. The shorter, curly style of her hair added a new maturity to her, yet at the same time suggested a youthful vibrancy that made her eyes and mouth appear as impish as they did seductive. *Achingly* seductive. She'd always been stunningly beautiful, but in their time apart she'd grown more so and, dear heavens, how he *wanted* her!

'I noticed your car was in the drive when we got back last night,' Taylor said, jolting his thoughts back to safer lines. 'How'd you manage that?'

He shifted in his chair in an effort to bring his body back to heel. 'Your coach organized it. If you give me his number after we get back from the specialist, I'll call and thank him.'

Her gaze widened. 'What do you mean, after *we* get back? I don't need—'

'Taylor... You just admitted you don't feel confident using the crutches. So don't try telling me now that you *want* to go the specialist under your own steam.' He smiled victoriously at her grunt of defeat. 'Since the Porsche doesn't make a good ambulance, I thought we'd take your car. Any objections?'

Taylor had plenty, but none of them had anything to do with his reasoning. 'Makes sense, I guess.'

'Oh, goody!' Melanie burst into the conversation. 'I'll ride in the front with you,' she told Craig.

'No, you'll ride in the back. Your mother will be in the front.'

'But I don't like riding in the back. I *never* ride in the back!'

'That's OK, Melanie,' Taylor soothed. 'I don't mind sitting in the back.'

'I don't believe children should ride in the front of the car while adults sit in the back, Taylor.'

She could tell Craig was determined not to give in on the subject. Technically he was right; it was bad manners. But Melanie was used to sitting up front if she was driving with either Liz or herself. She had rarely been in a car with anyone else except her grandparents, and they had always used a chauffeur. And she'd *never* been in a car with both her mother and her father at the same time. Taylor looked across at the pouting child; being with Craig was still very much a novelty to the five-year-old.

'Why don't you go wash your face and brush your teeth?' Taylor suggested, praying her daughter wasn't going to dig in her heels and argue the point. She doubted she was up to handling anything that difficult without bursting either into tears or a fit of temper.

Melanie took only a second to consider the idea before pushing her chair clear of the table and racing from the room. Bernie, as usual, followed in ungainly pursuit.

'You have to understand you're new to her, Craig,' Taylor said, not looking at him, but able to *feel* his gaze on her. 'Right now you're a toy she's not ready to share and she thinks you want to be with her as much as she wants to be with you.'

'I know exactly how she feels,' Craig said, capturing her attention, and she would have sworn every unbroken bone in her body melted under his hot brown gaze.

'Right now the only person I want to be with is her mother. And I'm not sure I'm ready to share, either.'

'I told you she was exactly like you,' she said huskily.

'You also once said that unlike me she wasn't a quitter.'

Taylor lowered her eyes as his words dragged the bitterness of the past too uncomfortably close, but determined fingers reached across the table to lift her chin.

'I'm not going to give you up again, Tay,' he warned. 'Even if it means I fight you *and* her every inch of the way.'

Though she was honest enough to admit Craig had triumphed over her heart twelve years ago, Melanie was too little to fight her battles alone; for that reason Taylor intended to be in her corner.

'Let's compromise,' she offered, not allowing Craig's sceptically raised eyebrow to intimidate her. 'I'll go with Liz to the surgery and Mel can go with you and sit in the front. On the way home, Melanie can sit in the back.'

'Your idea of compromising varies a hell of a lot from mine!' he said drily.

'There's no need to keep carrying me!' she protested as Craig deposited her onto the sofa after their trip to the specialist.

'Yes, there is. It's easier on my nerves than watching you struggle with those damn crutches!'

'Well, the more practice I get, the sooner I'll improve on them,' she reasoned, turning to see what he was doing in the kitchen. Her attention was distracted by the sight of Bernie bounding into the room closely followed by Melanie. He pounced straight up onto the sofa next to Taylor and nuzzled her face.

'It's good to see you, too, boy!' She laughed, trying to push the huge animal away. 'Mel, help me get him down!'

Craig stood back, watching the scene without comment, as together, mother and daughter wrestled with the enormous mass of fur, giggling with glee at their futile efforts to budge the beast. Clearly all three of them were enjoying themselves and he wondered how often they'd played this game. The ring of the phone interrupted the loud hilarity of the threesome and instinctively his hand reached for it.

'Hello... No, you have the right number. This is *Craig* Adams... Taylor's husband...' He grinned as Taylor leaned over the back of the sofa, glaring furiously at him for the way he'd identified himself.

'Who is it?' she asked, endeavouring to reach her crutches and push the dog away at the same time. Smiling at her efforts to get to her feet and ultimately the phone, he offered her no answer, continuing to speak with the caller.

'Unfortunately my wife can't come to the phone right now...'

Wife! The nerve of the man! Just because they'd never been divorced didn't mean he could go around calling her his wife! She glared at him as he explained how and why she was encased in plaster.

'Craig! *Who is it*?'

He covered the mouthpiece with his hand. 'A Karen Browning. Says her daughter, Renee, does ballet with Melanie and that you'd arranged to drop Mel over there today so they could play.'

'Oh, gosh! I forgot about it in all the confusion!'

'Can I go, Mummy? Can I?'

Taylor looked sadly at her daughter. 'Sorry, honey, but Mrs Browning doesn't drive and—' she motioned to her leg '—I can't—'

'Karen?' Craig was again speaking into the phone. 'Any problem if I drop Mel over in say... oh, twenty minutes?'

'Craig!'

Furious at the way he was assuming control of the situation, Taylor was on her feet and moving towards him with as much speed as she could manage—which wasn't much—and by the time she reached him, he'd replaced the receiver.

'Mel,' he said, 'I'll drive you over to Renee's place.'

'Now listen here, Craig!' Taylor's protest went unheeded.

'Run upstairs and pack whatever you need,' he told the little girl.

Eager to comply, Melanie leaped to her feet and ran past her mother without sparing her a second glance. Unfortunately so, too, did the large and lumbering St Bernard. The latter clipped the side of a crutch, thus sending Taylor scrambling to regain her balance. Trying to compensate her tilt to the right, she placed too much weight on the left crutch and it slipped away from her. Not even the lightning reflexes that enabled Craig to get close enough to grab her were enough to prevent her crashing to the floor and bringing him with her. After a few seconds of silence, muttered oaths filled the air.

'Are you all right? Taylor! Are you all right?'

Craig's voice was tinged with worry and she saw the same concern in his face, but Taylor was incapable of forming the words to dissipate it. The feel of his body pressed against her own sent her mental facilities into turmoil. It had been so long since she'd felt his weight upon her; so long since she'd looked up into his handsome face and seen genuine caring on it that the best she could manage was a dazed nod.

'What about the leg? Is it okay?'

Again she nodded, unable to prevent her hand rising to draw a finger along his slightly off-centre nose.

'Tay...'

Of their own accord, her fingers moved to trace his tiny scar before gliding along his cheek-bone and jaw; the slight roughness they encountered fascinated her as it had years ago. How could a man as gentle a lover as she knew Craig to be, be so hard, bristly and angular on the outside? Again her fingers played over the sculptured planes of his face.

Beneath her touch, Craig felt as if he were catching fire. He closed his eyes in an effort to regain some control, but it didn't work. Too much heat was radiating from the woman beneath him; too many hot, passionate memories screened in his head. With a soft curse, he gave up the token fight.

A shiver shook Taylor's whole body as he lowered his head and moved his moist mouth against her neck. Instinctively she arched closer and brought her arms around him to reduce the distance between them even more, just the weight of him exciting her more than she would have believed possible. Desperately she twisted her head to force his mouth to hers and was rewarded for her efforts by the wild, familiar dampness of his tongue against her own. But this was no tentative, uncertain reunion. It was full on passion and too-long penned-up desire. It was life and death, want and need; each hungry, hurried movement was a reaction to a deeply instinctive desire and a prelude to another.

She held his head tightly between her hands, not wanting to ever again be bereft of this man's mouth or the sensations his kiss aroused within her. As the ferocity of their movements against each other worked the back of her shirt free, she marvelled at the coolness of the slate against her skin and the stark contrast it presented to the sensual flames ignited in her blood by the touch and taste of Craig.

While her tongue delighted in a provocative battle with his, far away she could hear someone whispering her name. Its urgency was trying to distract her from the glory of the oral duel she was enjoying. She wished it gone! Wanting and needing nothing but more of the man who held her...

'Mummy! Mummmeeee! Mummeee!' Slowly the insistent calling penetrated her clouded brain. When it did, it acted with the speed and effect of a circuit-breaker on Taylor's passion.

'Get off me!' she demanded, trying to shove free of the mass of masculine muscle pinning her to the floor. She fought both for freedom and much-needed oxygen for her lungs. 'Get off! Mel's calling!'

Craig stilled and looked at her for long moments before the meaning of her words hit him. Muttering an oath, he eased himself onto his feet, pinching the bridge of his nose between thumb and forefinger in the vague hope of regulating his breathing. Or, at the very least, diffusing the irritation he felt at having his dream snatched from his grasp.

'You could at least help me up!' Taylor accused, the child's voice persisting from the level above them. 'All right! All right! I'm coming, Melanie! Just hang on a second, will you?'

Judging by the impatient tone Taylor used to answer her daughter, Craig wasn't the only one irritated at the interruption, he noted. Pleased, he helped her to her feet, then, steadying her with a grip on her forearm, reached down and picked up the crutches. The slight tremble of her body and her irregular breathing brought him added satisfaction; Taylor had been as aroused as he.

'Given your current physical and emotional state, it might be safer if I carried you up the stairs,' he said.

She paused in the act of positioning the crutches under her arms to bestow a narrowed-eyed glare at him. 'Like hell it would!'

Taylor lay quietly on her bed examining the eggshell-blue ceiling above her. Physically she was exhausted from the events of the previous night and today, but, as sensible as an afternoon nap had seemed, it was impossible to achieve. There were too many things she had to work out, not the least her feelings for Craig. Actually *they* were her biggest problem, but not, she admitted, her most pressing one.

She had to find a housekeeper. *And fast*! Then there was the problem of getting Melanie to and from school. She could possibly ask the mother of one of Mel's friends, but the only one she really knew was Karen Browning, and Renee went to a different school. As yet, Taylor hadn't met the mothers of any of Melanie's classmates and she wasn't at all comfortable about asking total strangers to put themselves out. Hell! Why did she have to injure herself before she was properly settled in Sydney? Not that she would have been thrilled at being incapacitated at any time, but three months from now would certainly have been more *convenient*!

The muted burr of the bedroom telephone severed her bout of self-pity and she stared at it, somehow knowing who it would be. She didn't dwell on the spark of excitement the thought triggered in her.

'Hello, Craig,' she said before giving the caller time to identify himself.

'Very good!' he praised. 'Your powers of perception are excellent!'

'It was either you or Liz, and the way my luck is running I wasn't stupid enough to think it would be her.'

'Ouch!' he said with amusement. 'What are you doing?'

'Well, I've just finished a torrid game of squash and I'm about to start painting the ceiling! What do you think I'm doing? Nothing! Which is about all I *will* be able to do for the next month!'

'Poor Taylor!'

'Save your pity. I can provide my own. In abundance.'

'Well, maybe I can cheer you up. I called to let you know I'm picking Melanie up at about six, then I'll be over to fix dinner.'

'I'm not hungry.' She had no intention of being alone with him.

'You have to eat.'

'I don't have to if I'm not hungry,' she said stubbornly.

'I'm sure Melanie will be hungry. Or do you only feed her when you feed yourself?'

'Of course not! But even with my leg in a cast, I think I can manage to scramble some eggs!'

'And you also think you'll be able to manage feeding that overgrown pony you call a dog?' he enquired in a facetious tone. 'He nearly trampled *me* last night in his haste to empty his dinner dish. Think you can fend him off? As I recall, your efforts earlier today left a lot to be desired. In more ways than one, I might add.'

The less-than-subtle reference to the kiss they'd shared caused a stirring in her lower abdomen she knew better than to acknowledge, but he gave her no chance anyway.

'See you at six, Tay.'

He hung up before she could say another word. She should have been furious with his take-charge attitude, but the sound of his voice had triggered far more disturbing emotions than anger.

Taylor had acknowledged from the beginning that moving back to Sydney would mean confronting Craig, but she hadn't expected things to be so difficult. For one thing, she'd thought herself mature enough to deal with meeting him on an impersonal basis if he chose to play a part in Melanie's life. But she'd been wrong. *Dead* wrong. The emotions she'd experienced since seeing him again were deeply personal!

She recognized all the neon signs of lust—the raging hormones, the escalating pulse and the shivers of awareness. And she might have been able to ignore them had it not been for the other, less conspicuous, but far more dangerous signs she was reading in her body; the need to have Craig simply *hold* her, the need to touch his hair, the need to hear him say he *believed* she hadn't deliberately planned Melanie's conception. These *needs* were reactions that worried her. They were signs that warned her she was still in love with him, that winning his trust still mattered.

She wished she could genuinely claim to hate Craig, but she couldn't. Oh, sure, over the years she'd said the words, but as the old adage claimed, actions spoke louder than words, and crying oneself to sleep every night for the first two years after one left a man wasn't the action of a woman consumed by hate. Loneliness, hurt and confusion, maybe, but not hate. And the gradual cessation of those tears over the next three years didn't mean one had progressed into the blissful state of indifference, either, as this past week had shown.

Opening the drawer of her bedside table, she withdrew the photograph of Craig she'd never been able to bring herself to throw away. For a long time, she'd told herself she kept it out so that Melanie would have a face to identify with the word *father*, but she knew now her heart hadn't been fooled.

CHAPTER EIGHT

CRAIG arrived armed with two huge brown grocery bags and a cheerful Melanie in tow.

'Since Mel and I are cooking dinner, we stopped off and picked up a few things,' he explained. 'And we also got you a video to watch.'

On cue and wearing a grin, Melanie held up the item and Taylor forced herself to look at it rather than the way the weight of the grocery bags highlighted the muscles in Craig's tanned forearms.

'Eh, thanks.' She noted the title despite the rabid urging of her hormones to cast her eyes back to the grocery bags. She smiled. 'I'll watch it later.'

'No, Mummy! Watch it *now*. So you don't get in our way.'

Laughing, Craig sent Taylor a quizzical look. 'Am I wrong or are your own words coming back to haunt you?'

Reluctant to spoil Melanie's eagerness to begin her first father-daughter culinary experience, Taylor allowed herself to be banished to the sofa. But although the movie was one she'd wanted to see, her concentration was marred by the muted sounds of Craig's voice and the high-pitched giggles of her daughter drifting from the kitchen. She glanced over her shoulder to the shutters above the breakfast bar, which Melanie had closed because 'dinner is going to be a s'prise', feeling hurt that her daughter had so cheerfully excluded her from the activities. Annoyed with her pettiness, she produced her most delighted smile when Melanie raced in and an-

90

nounced, 'Dinner is served!' before quickly scampering off to the dining room.

Having flicked off the video with the remote, she was working to get to her feet when Craig materialized at her side, causing her heart, if not her feet, to trip.

'Leave the crutches. I'll carry you.'

'No thanks, I can manage.' She continued in her less-than-graceful efforts to stand, knowing amused brown eyes watched her every move. Once upright with the crutches safely positioned under her arms, she gave a triumphant smile.

'Such dexterity! An intoxicated octopus has nothing on you.' His teasing tone tightened her stomach in a way too reminiscent of a time when light-hearted banter had often led to impromptu lovemaking. Shoving the disturbing thought aside, she gave him a bored look.

'You're blocking my way.'

He stepped aside, and, executing a half bow, he waved his hand towards the dining room. 'After you.'

'Such chivalry,' she said drily.

'Chivalry? Nah! I just happen to love looking at your cute ass!'

This time, as the crutches went in all directions, Craig's hand arrived in time to steady her.

'Still think you can manage on your own?'

'*You* caused that!' she snapped, embarrassment and anger leaving no room for gratitude. 'What are you trying to do, ensure I have another fall?'

'I am if it ends up like the one we had earlier today.'

'Don't get your hopes up! This morning I was concussed!'

He laughed. 'But you didn't hit your head.'

'No, but I'll hit yours if you don't shut up!' Honestly, he was driving her crazy! Agitated, she moved with as much speed as was possible to the dining room.

Melanie's excited chatter about the afternoon spent with Renee was the accompanying course to the seafood pasta. While on the plus side, her daughter's non-stop monologue alleviated the need for Taylor to converse with the man seated opposite, the negative was that it prolonged both the meal and Craig's presence. And the longer the meal went on, the harder it was not to covertly study him. Already her gaze had taken in every detail of the hard, muscular body visible above the table, right down to his soft, indecently long eyelashes that lay in perfect dark crescents against his skin when he lowered his eyes. On an intellectual level, she told herself, none of these things affected her, but while her brain was being practical, her femininity was flashing a red alert. Bit by bit she felt her composure crumbling. Much more of this and she was either going to have some sort of bizarre hormonal seizure or a nervous breakdown!

'... and Renee's got this real big panda. She calls him Sam. Isn't that a dumb name for a panda? I think a panda should be called something that starts with *P*! Like Peter or Pepe or Pa—'

'Melanie!' When two pairs of startled eyes focused on her, Taylor realized she sounded more tense than she'd intended and quickly moderated her tone. 'Your dinner is getting cold. Stop talking and *eat.*'

'I don't want to eat any more. I'm full.'

'Nonsense. You've barely touched it.'

'So?' The tone and look were insolent. 'I don't have to eat it if I don't want to—'

'Melanie. You *know* the rules. No room for dinner, no dessert.'

'But, Mummeee,' the child whined, 'I don't—'

'Eat!' Craig's loud command caused both females to physically jump and he instantly wished the word back. Mel was looking at him like he was an axe murderer and Tay's rigid expression showed she wasn't thrilled with his heavy-handed attempt at parenting, either.

He muttered a general 'Sorry.' Then he turned his attention to the child. 'I didn't mean to shout at you,

Melanie. But you shouldn't speak to your mother like that. What say you eat half of what's left on your plate and then you can go dish up the dessert we made, huh?'

'For me, too?' she asked dubiously.

'*Only* if you eat at least half of what you've got left,' he repeated, thinking it sounded like a pretty reasonable deal to him.

Melanie flicked her hair over her shoulders, then reached for her fork while flashing him a five-year-old's beautiful smile. 'OK, Daddy.'

A tide of pleasure raced through him and he was overwhelmed by the sense of achievement his daughter's positive response generated. Even when he'd pulled off his first multimillion-dollar deal, he hadn't experienced such a charge of amazement at his success. At least then he'd been armed with an honours degree in business; with Melanie he'd been going on pure instinct. *He, Craig Adams, had tried paternal reasoning with his daughter and come up trumps with nothing to go on but his own feelings!*

He looked across to share his pleasure with Taylor, but her head was bent intently over her plate and no matter how much he mentally urged her to lift it, she didn't. But he wasn't content to rely on telepathy alone.

'How is it, Tay?'

'Fine.'

'Just *fine*?' His persistence brought her gaze to his.

'OK, it's excellent,' she conceded as if irritated by the fact. 'But you always were a better cook than me.'

He laughed. 'Melanie's a better cook than you.'

Though her daughter giggled, Taylor sent him a bored look over the rim of her glass of Chablis. 'Pathetic though my cooking may be by your standards, gourmet meals aren't essential to survival. There is nutritional value even in something as simple as baked beans.'

'Yuck!' Melanie exclaimed. 'I *hate* baked beans!'

'Well, you better start *not* hating them, young lady,' Taylor advised. 'Because until I can find a housekeeper, you might be getting them on a regular basis. I'm not crazy about standing over a hot stove suspended on crutches!' She looked at Craig. 'I suppose it's too much to hope Adams Relief has branched out into domestic staff?'

'Nope. Domestic staff's too unpredictable. You send a brilliant cook out to do a few weeks' temporary work for a client and then what happens?' He shook his head. 'The ingrate offers her a fantastic salary and hires her off your payroll! That kind of poaching doesn't make it worthwhile.

'*Although*,' he said, 'there is a simpler solution.'

Taylor didn't trust the gleam dancing in his eyes or the fact he'd practically read her mind. 'Such as?'

'I could come over and cook dinner each night it—'

'Yeah!' shouted Melanie. 'And then I could help you and—'

Face Craig every single night? '*No way!*' she said, aghast.

'Why not? I have to eat anyway and it would give me a chance to spend more time with Melanie.'

'It. . . it would be too disruptive for her—'

'What's disrup—*disrapatave* mean?' Taylor ignored her daughter's question, stunned that Craig could have suggested such a thing in front of the child.

'It means, Melanie,' he said, looking straight at Taylor, 'that Mummy thinks it's not a good idea.'

'But *why*, Mummy?'

Seeing her daughter's disappointment made Taylor feel like the Wicked Witch of the West.

'Well, Craig, eh. . .*Daddy*,' she corrected, 'works very long hours. Sometimes he stays at the office until very late or. . .or has to go to business dinners and things. That means he wouldn't be able to cook dinner before it was time for you to go to bed.'

'Not a problem,' Craig said. 'I can finish any time I like. In fact, I'm only too happy to fit in with Melanie's schedule.'

Taylor glared at him. 'That's very generous of you, but it's not only meals that have to be considered. And since I'll need to employ someone to take Melanie to and from school, I might as—'

'No reason I can't do that, too.'

Melanie's unfettered cheer of delight was deafening. Damn! *He was doing it again*! Using Melanie to manipulate *her*! Fighting hard not to create a scene in front of her daughter, Taylor drew a steadying breath before speaking.

'Craig, you're being ridiculous. What happens if you get held up in a meeting or something and Mel's left waiting at the school alone? Plus you'd have to drop her off in the morning an hour before school started to make the office on time. *Plus*,' she said loudly when it was evident he was about to say something, 'your office is in the city and your apartment is miles away on the other side of the harbour. You'd spend all your time in your car in peak-hour traffic.'

His grimace of distaste told her she had him stymied. The knowledge was enough to bring a smug smile to her lips and she couldn't resist adding with pseudo graciousness, 'Generous as your offer is, Craig, it just isn't practical with you living so far away.'

'He could stay here.'

Melanie's words made her the focus of both adults' stunned attention. 'Please,' she implored, tears streaming down her face. 'Please let him stay. Then I could have a *real* daddy...just for a little while....'

Craig's gaze shifted to Taylor. 'Well,' he said. 'What do you think...?'

CHAPTER NINE

'HAVE you ever considered a lobotomy?' Liz asked.

'I've heard they're dangerous,' Taylor replied, twisting the cord of the phone restlessly between her fingers.

'As far as you're concerned, my girl, they're a damn sight less dangerous than Craig Adams! I should have X-rayed your thick skull instead of your knee! What possessed you to let him move in?'

Sighing, Taylor leaned back against the breakfast bar. 'I didn't *let* him move in. I just couldn't come up with a reason *not* to let him. At least not one I could have sold to Melanie.'

'Jeez, Taylor, the kid still believes in Santa Claus. *Anything* would have done!'

Remembering her daughter's heartbreaking plea, Taylor had to blink back tears. 'No, it wouldn't have, Liz. Besides,' she said, trying to sound comfortable with her decision, 'it's not as if we're sleeping together or anything. He's in the spare room upstairs and I've moved into the downstairs one. Everything's been fine so far.'

'*So far*.' Liz's tone was ominous. 'I blame myself for this,' she continued. 'If I hadn't had to attend this stupid medical conference, I'd have been there to protect you from yourself *and* your ex.'

'He's not my *ex*.'

'Is that supposed to *reassure* me?' Liz paused then resumed in a softer voice. 'Look, I'll be over to see you as soon as I get back to Sydney, but if you need me for anything in the meantime, anything at all, call me. OK?'

'Thanks, Liz, but I'll be fine. I can handle this. I'm more mature and a lot more sensible than I was at eighteen.'

'Kiddo, you've *never* been sensible where *that* guy was concerned!'

Replacing the phone and staring out the kitchen window to where Craig was playing with Melanie, Taylor feared her friend was right. Every sane, sensible bone in her body seemed to have disappeared the moment Craig had come back into her life. In the ten days since he'd moved into her house on the pretence of helping out and getting to know Melanie, Taylor's emotions had been jumping all over the place. One minute she was convinced he'd cleverly manipulated her; the next she suspected he was as reluctant to be in the situation as she and doing it strictly for Melanie's sake.

Perhaps, she thought, taking a glass from the sink and filling it with water, Liz's suggestion of a lobotomy was one to be considered. Lord knew Craig Adams was driving her insane! His presence seemed to both crowd her and leave her lonely, depending on whether she was trying to ignore the effect he had on her body when they were in the same room, or trying to ignore it as she lay in bed sleepless and alone, knowing he was in the bedroom upstairs. Equally alone.

Resting her weight on one crutch, she sipped the water, contemplating the father-and-daughter scene beyond the window. One thing was certain—Melanie had never been happier. Used to being the sole focus of her daughter's admiration, a sudden flash of jealousy cramped her heart. Disgusted with herself, Taylor grabbed for the other crutch, forgetting she still held the glass. She screamed as it crashed onto the slate floor, splintering in all directions; anger and frustration exploded within her at the sight of the wet mess.

'Taylor! Taylor, where are you? Are you OK?'

'Oh, yeah!' she snapped. 'I'm great! Just great!' For some reason, the concern etched on Craig's face as he raced into the adjoining family room made her burst into tears. 'I broke a glass!' she wailed.

'Is *that* all? I thought you'd hurt yourself.'

'*All*? I'm so flaming useless I can't even get myself a drink of water without help!'

'Aw, honey!'

'Don't come...' She started to sob a warning, but he was already carefully picking a barefoot path around the debris.

'A broken glass is not the end of the world.' He brushed the tears from her cheeks with his thumbs, tilting her head so she looked up into liquid brown eyes. 'And you are *not* useless. You're clever and bright and...beautiful.'

'None of which gets me a glass of water,' she complained. 'It—'

'They'll get you,' he interrupted, ensnaring her chin and thus her gaze, 'anything you want, Tay. At least with me.'

Her heart was again pushing blood too quickly through her body and disrupting her breathing. She knew it was because he was so close and touching her. She lifted her hands and grasped his wrists to ward him off, but her good intentions were sidetracked by the warmth and latent strength she felt beneath his skin. The urge to continue her tactile exploration up his forearms was too powerful to deny; her execution of the act drew him nearer.

She told herself to step away, but greedily grasped at the knowledge that without her crutches she'd risk a fall. So she remained still, endangering her heart to save her body. A body so close to Craig's she'd have sworn her sigh was responsible for the rise and fall of his chest.

'Tay...'

She closed her eyes as he reached a tentative hand to her hair, her spine tingling as eager fingers burrowed through the locks to brace her head. Anticipating the arrival of his mouth, her lips parted, yet the erotic surprise of his thumb caressing the sensitive flesh of her lower lip made her stomach drop, her heart flip. And after his finger had tormented her with three insidiously slow strokes, there was no way she could stop her teeth from stilling it, or her tongue from rolling across and around it. His gasped response vaulted her to a sensuous high, which engulfed her, demanding she repeat the action. She did. Again and again. The ridged hardness of fingernail and warm heat of skin triggered phallic fantasies in her head and poured liquid heat into her womb.

'Did you hurt yourself, Daddy?'

Taylor's jaw fell slack as Melanie's voice hit like a bucket of ice water; she clutched frantically at the sink as Craig stepped away from her.

'Well, did you?' the child persisted, looking from one mute adult to the other.

'Hurt myself?' Craig's bemused expression told Taylor he was nearly as disorientated as she was, the difference being he at least could speak. *She* couldn't even breathe.

'Yes. When *I* hurt myself, Mummy always kisses me,' the little girl told him. 'Wasn't that what Mummy was doing? Kissing you better?'

Craig looked from daughter to mother and back again, before enlightenment lit his features. 'Oh, yeah, Mel!' he said with feeling. 'I happen to think your mummy kisses better than anyone I've ever known.'

Later when Craig asked if Taylor minded if he went to the office after dinner to catch up on some work, she was so awash with relief she'd practically shoved him out the door!

Now, with Melanie asleep, she settled her head back against the cool leather of the sofa. She was grateful for the solitude and the time out from her daughter's *Daddy this* and *Daddy that* and the chance to corral her erratic hormones, which had been running amok since the episode in the kitchen. She didn't dare speculate on what might have—correction, *would* have happened but for Mel's interruption. And what worried her was that Mel's presence was no longer as effective a buffer as it had been a week ago. It didn't nullify the dangerous thoughts and sensations that crept through Taylor each morning as she faced Craig, clean-shaven and shower damp, across the breakfast table; nor did it stop her heart from fluttering at the sound of his car pulling into the drive a little after three each day. And with her daughter at school, there was nothing at all during the hours in between to prevent Taylor's unoccupied mind from conjuring up images of the man and flicking through the memories of their past passion.

Caught up in her thoughts, it wasn't until Bernie staggered to his feet that she realized a key was turning in the front door. Her heart thumped and her eyes darted to the wall clock; it wasn't even nine o'clock! He'd said he'd be *late*. Unable to escape to her room without meeting him, she forced herself to appear unperturbed by his arrival.

'Hi,' she said with false brightness. 'You're back early.'

'Yeah, I am. Want a coffee?'

'Mmmm, thanks.'

'What's all this?'

She twisted on the couch so she could look across into the kitchen and saw him frowning at the full but no doubt by now lukewarm percolator. 'Oh, I made myself one earlier, but couldn't manage to carry it from the kitchen so I had to drink it where I poured it.' She shrugged. 'I lost interest in a second cup.'

'You really hate not being fully mobile and able to function normally, don't you?'

'Now there's an understatement!' she retorted. 'And I'm getting bored out of my brain! I've had a gutful of daytime soap operas, I'm sick of reading and playing patience and a person can only listen to music for so long! I'm dying from inactivity and I can't even look for work because I can't drive! It seems like I spend all my time lying in bed, sitting on my backside and hanging between two pieces of wood twenty-four hours a day!'

'Cheer up, Tay. You'll have had the cast on two weeks tomorrow. That means there're only two more weeks to go.'

'Might as well be forever! I can't *stand* this. The sooner things are back to normal round here, the better...' Her words faltered.

'The better you'll like it,' he finished.

The lifeless tone of his voice left her chilled. Then again, perhaps it wasn't his tone, but the words themselves. Once the cast was gone, so was Craig. *That* was normal, but in all honesty would she like it better?

He set two mugs of coffee on the table along with a dish of chocolate mints. At her questioning eyebrow, he smiled. 'Picked them up on the way home.'

She plucked two from the dish and grinned. 'In that case, I'm glad you finished your work early.'

His mouth tightened and he lowered himself onto the seat next to her; elbows on knees, he interlocked his fingers and stared at the floor. 'I didn't go to the office to work, Taylor.' He turned his head towards her; his features were taut, though a thoughtful frown wrinkled his forehead. 'I went there to think.'

Taylor swallowed hard and fast; apprehension overpowered the sweet tang of peppermint in her mouth. She didn't want to get into a deep and meaningful conversation with him. Not now. Not with Mel upstairs asleep. Not with the room lit only by the glow of the television. It was too intimate, too tempting. Her mind raced for diversionary conversation.

'Peace and quiet are pretty scarce with Mel around. She—'

'It's not peace and quiet I want,' he interrupted. 'It's peace of mind.'

His intensity alarmed her. 'I don't understand what you mean.'

Craig stood up and crossed to the far side of the room. He recognized her response for the stalling tactic it was, but suddenly his decision to be totally honest with Taylor carried too high a price tag. She'd throw him out and never let him back into her life. Hers or Melanie's. And today he'd realized being a part of their life, if only as a part-time father to Mel, was vital to his existence. He didn't kid himself that he had been, or ever could be, essential to theirs, but he couldn't return to the delusional ignorance-is-bliss lifestyle he'd been maintaining for the last half decade.

What he was about to tell Taylor amounted to emotional suicide, but he was in a catch-22 situation—damned if he did and equally damned if he didn't.

'What I'm talking about is guilt, Taylor. Guilt so paralysing and all-consuming it chokes me every time I look at Melanie. A guilt that's ten thousand times worse when she lifts those big brown eyes of hers and smiles and calls me Daddy.' He sighed, knowing every word made his hope for a future with this woman more remote. 'I never *earned* the title, Taylor. I *inherited* it.'

Amusement danced on her face. 'Yeah, well, that's the usual way it happens, Craig. Except I guess in adoption cases.'

'I'm not talking biology here. Besides, an adoptive father sires a child in his heart, so it's the same anyway.' Ignoring the startled look his comment drew, he continued. 'The thing is, fathers are supposed to *believe* in their kids. No matter what. And I never did that, yet I've inherited a healthy, happy little girl who...'

A worrying thought stemmed his voice. Doctors had warned that due to her premature birth and the subsequent treatments required, Melanie might be deaf or blind, or suffer chronic health problems and learning disabilities in later life. Suddenly it occurred to him he'd accepted Melanie's good health at face value.

'She *is* healthy, isn't she, Taylor? I mean—'

Taylor nodded quickly. 'Oh, yeah! She's fine! *Truly*.' She was beaming with maternal pride as she unwrapped another mint. 'Mel was a real fighter from the start. But there isn't a day goes by I don't thank God for being in her corner.'

'God wasn't the only one there, Tay.' The scratchy quality of Craig's voice fell uncomfortably on her ears. 'You spent every waking minute and I suspect every sleeping one, as well, believing she would live. I couldn't do that. I wasn't there for her.'

She felt guilt for his guilt. 'Look, I know I gave you a hard time for not going and seeing her more often, but...' She paused, realizing what she was saying was coming five years too late. 'I understand now how you felt. Liz told me how upsetting you found it seeing her hooked up to all that machinery and—'

Craig shook his head. 'Liz was covering my miserable ass so as not to upset you even more. The truth is, seeing her on those machines didn't bother me.'

'It...it *didn't*?' She couldn't comprehend how he could make such a statement. She'd felt as if she were dying a little each time she walked into the hospital.

'I didn't get upset, Tay, because I *never* went to see her. Until the day you brought her to my office, I'd never set eyes on my daughter!'

CHAPTER TEN

'YOU swine!'

Rage and disbelief brought Taylor to her feet, where she teetered unsteadily, the soft padded leather of the sofa arm providing her with only limited support.

'Be care—'

'Don't you come near me!' she shouted, seeing him take a step in her direction. 'Keep the hell away!'

'Shhh! Quiet down or you'll wake Mel.'

A brittle, bitter laugh broke from her. 'Oh, that's rich! You don't give a damn about Melanie! *Your daughter was critically ill and you didn't care enough to even look at her*. Not even *once*, damn you!'

'Taylor, it wasn't like that! I swear! *Please*,' he begged. 'Let me explain.'

'*Explain*? How the hell can you explain turning away from your own daughter? You *told* me you were going to see her. You let me believe you *had*.' Stray tears began slipping under her guard. 'Why, Craig? Why the pretence? Why the lies?'

'Because I didn't expect her to live! Hell, Taylor, no one did except you!'

'But she was our daughter! *Your* daughter.'

'That wasn't enough to guarantee she'd live! The doctors said that—'

'I can't believe you wrote your own child off as being a statistic simply because everyone else did! But then again—' she shot him a disgusted look '—you'd never wanted a child, so I guess you figured the odds were in your favour!'

'That's a rotten thing to say! I never wished her dead! God, Taylor, cut me some slack here,' he pleaded.

Never in his life had Craig known desperation such as he felt now. He knew he deserved every bit of the disgust and loathing Taylor's eyes whipped him with, but he prayed that somewhere in her heart she'd have enough pity for him to at least let him explain. Pity was something he'd always despised, but now it was his only hope.

'Please, Taylor, it wasn't because I'd been against us having children. It wasn't because I didn't want her to live. It was because of you—'

'Me! You're trying to blame—'

'No! I'm not trying to place blame anywhere except where it belongs. With me. I'm simply trying to explain, make you understand—'

He stopped. She'd covered her ears with her hands and was violently shaking her head.

He knew then he was fighting a losing battle; knew in fact the battle was *already* lost. Whatever Taylor had once felt for him was gone and nothing he said now could revive it. Had he not told her the truth he might have had a chance, but he hadn't been able to endure the guilt.

Yet this time, instead of sitting back and accepting what fate dished up because he felt he deserved it, just as he'd done when Taylor walked out on him, he *was* going to fight. Because even if he didn't deserve a daughter, Melanie deserved a father with more guts and loyalty than he'd shown in the past.

He stared out the sliding doors leading to the patio. His reflection and that of Taylor's behind him was muted, as night turned the glass into a muddy mirror. But he knew darkness wasn't only synonymous with night.

'All right, Craig,' Taylor said, surprising him. '*Explain*.'

He spun around prepared to thank her, but she gave him no chance.

'*Explain* how you could cold-bloodedly turn your back on your daughter. But *don't*,' she warned, 'delude yourself that you'll ever be able to make me understand.'

The bitterness in her voice froze his vocal cords.

'Come on,' she pushed, 'let's hear your fabulous explanation.'

Only the knowledge of how much she was hurting—hurting because of him—stopped him from telling her to shut up! But he still sent up a dozen silent apologies for the inclination. Then he cleared his throat and began at what for him was the beginning.

'While it's true I was angry when you got pregnant, after a bit I started thinking about the baby, about us having a family, and I kind of got used to the idea. Well, a little anyway,' he qualified. 'And I started to think that maybe things weren't going to be all that bad. That there was a chance we wouldn't go the way of my parents, but be like yours, able to keep the baby separate from ourselves. I know that was simply the lesser of two evils, but it let me hope a child didn't mean I was going to lose you.' Closing his eyes, he forced himself to concentrate only on what had to be said and not to venture down sidetracks leading to what he knew now had only been pipedreams.

'But almost simultaneously, things started going wrong. You were constantly sick and crying and so bad-tempered all the time, I got the feeling you didn't want me around. I know you denied it,' he said, quickly anticipating an interjection that didn't come. 'But that's how it seemed to me, and well, it put me right back to square one where the idea of a baby was concerned. And then . . .' He drew a long breath. 'Then I arrived home that day and found you haemorrhaging.'

The room was so silent Craig glanced over his shoulder to make sure she was still listening, that she hadn't already walked away. She lowered her eyes from him and the pain was like a kick in the guts. He turned back to the doors.

'Seeing you in hospital—in agony, bravely trying to fight off labour—nearly killed me, Taylor. I'd never felt so helpless in my life. You think you feel useless being in that cast? Well, it was a million times worse for me.'

'It was no picnic for me, either, you know!'

Her outburst caused him to pivot around. 'You think I didn't know that?' He swore, knowing he'd sounded defensive when he had no right. Several steadying breaths later he continued.

'Anyway, when I got the call to go to the hospital, I was at a meeting across town. I didn't trust myself to drive so I jumped in a taxi. It was peak hour and the traffic was horrendous. The driver did his best, but by the time I got there, you were already in theatre and they wouldn't let me in. I pleaded with the senior sister, but it was no go. She told me that under the circumstances I'd be more support to my wife if I remained calm because you would need me to lean on.

'I asked her what she meant,' he continued. 'And she told me that it was highly unlikely the baby would survive more than a few hours. And . . . and that was when I fell apart. I cried, Taylor. For the first time in my life, I cried. Not for the baby who wouldn't make it, but for *you*, because I knew how much you wanted that child. I didn't want to believe what the nurse told me, so I asked your doctor. He agreed the chances of Melanie coming home from hospital were worse than slim, but that you wouldn't accept that. He told me *I* should. That I *had* to.'

For Craig the memories accompanying his words made it hard for him to remain objective. He paused, rubbing his eyes as if somehow to disperse them. *He had to remain objective.*

'I knew how much you wanted that baby and how losing it would destroy you. I wanted to be there for you when that happened. I thought if I saw the baby I'd run the risk of forming an attachment that would ultimately lead to heartache and if that happened how much support could I give you? And—' he swallowed hard and turned back to face her '—and that's when I decided it would be wiser if I never saw her. Not even once.'

'Wiser? Or just *easier*?' she challenged.

'The past five years have shown it was neither. But, believe me, Taylor,' he said huskily, 'I've never regretted my decision more than I do now. When I... when I look at Melanie, it damn near kills me.'

Something in the urgency of his plea threatened to turn her anger to tears, but she fought to hang on to her fury. 'What is it you expect me to say, Craig? *Let's forgive and forget*?'

'No!' The denial was swift and firm. 'I just wanted you to know the truth. And despite the fact on some level I'll probably always see Melanie as the catalyst in your leaving me, you must believe that I genuinely care for her. Hell, Taylor, how could I not? She's your daughter.'

Her head jerked up at his words. 'You still don't understand, do you? Melanie's a person in her own right, Craig! She's not an appendage to me, not some kind of accessory!' She shook her head. 'This isn't going to work.'

Cold dread clutched him. 'What isn't?'

'Your staying here. We both know you're more interested in resurrecting our relationship than in forming a new one with your daughter.'

'That's not true!' He sighed. 'It might have been at first,' he admitted. 'But not any more. I'm not seeking the impossible any more, simply a chance to redeem myself.'

She had no time to ponder the tiny ache his declaration caused her, because he was speaking again. Even more urgently.

'Please, Taylor, let me try to make up for not being there for Melanie all those years ago. Please, let me stay. I promised her I'd stay till your leg was better. Don't force me to break that promise. Give me the chance to get to know her, to earn her trust.'

She wanted to scream *no*! No, because you don't deserve the chance to know her! No, because *you* didn't trust me! And no, because I'm scared she'll come to love you, that you might come to love her and I'm not sure I can bear to share either of you with—

Taylor was so shocked and disgusted by her thoughts that she started trembling. What was happening to her? Dear God, when had she become so selfish and insecure that she'd punish her own daughter by denying her what she wanted most—*a real father... just for a little while*?

'OK,' she said hurriedly, in a desperate attempt to avenge herself in her own eyes. 'You can stay.'

Across the room, Craig's entire body seemed to sag with relief. 'Thank you.'

'But only until the cast comes off,' she told him. 'Not one day longer.' Placing her crutches securely under her arms, she started from the room, then halted. She didn't look at him. 'I want you to know I'm doing this for Melanie's sake. *Not yours.*'

'I know that.'

During the next week, Craig spent as much time as he could with Melanie, but the truth was, as good as his intentions were, he was working blind when it came to knowing what a father was expected to do. Call him cynical, he thought, drawing the razor down his cheek, but he had a hunch it went beyond Mel's belief that daddies were only expected to supply junk food, toys and games on demand.

His grin caused him to nick himself with the blade and he swore. A sound of disapproval brought his head instantly from the mirror.

'You shouldn't say that word, Daddy.'

'Sorry, but if you hadn't barged in without knocking, you wouldn't have heard it,' he pointed out.

'You still shouldn't say it even if I'm not here,' she countered, in a way that marked her as a future lawyer. '*I'm* not allowed to say that word.' She gave him no time for further comment. 'Mummy told me to come up here and start my bath. Can I?' she asked. 'She said she'd come up in a little while and wash my hair, but I guess she didn't know you were in here.'

'I'll bet,' Craig said drily. Yep, a kid this sharp seemed destined for a law career! Then again, even blind Freddy would have seen how Taylor was going out of her way to avoid him. 'Go ahead and run your bath, Mel,' he said gently. 'I won't be long.'

Clad only in a terry robe, Melanie stood gazing at his foamed face with fascination, then nodded. Craig turned back to the mirror to continue his task.

'The other word I'm not allowed to say is the F-word,' his daughter continued conversationally, turning on the taps and pouring a heavy-handed amount of bubble bath into the tub. 'You know, f—'

'Melanie!' Craig dropped the razor into the sink and crouched down to her height. 'Where the devil did you hear language like that?'

'School.'

'*School*!' So much for Taylor thinking the exorbitant fees she paid for her daughter's education were warranted!

'It's OK, Daddy,' she said solemnly. 'I'd *never* say it.'

He was about to point out that she'd come damned close to it, but the sight of her tiny hand hesitantly lifting towards his jaw froze the words in his throat.

'Can...can I touch it?' she asked.

Her eyes were more imploring than her words, and her smile when Craig nodded caused his heart to constrict. She placed a tentative finger to the shaving cream and giggled when it came away coated in foam. The sound seemed to tinkle within the confines of the tiled bathroom and Craig found it almost melodious. Her hand returned to his face, but this time traced the area below his left eye.

'How'd you get this?' she asked.

'When I was about thirteen I got hit with a bat playing cricket. The stitches left a scar.'

She shook her dark head. 'Mummy says they aren't scars. They're bravery badges.'

He laughed. 'Bravery badges?'

'Mmm. See, I've got some, too.' She pulled open her robe and indicated a series of tiny marks around both her nipples. 'You know... I got them when I was a baby from all those machines that were plugged into me.'

Craig froze. He couldn't move, he couldn't speak, he couldn't breathe. All he could do was hear Melanie's words and *feel*. And what he felt was ripping his guts and heart out.

'Mummy says they're bravery badges because if I hadn't been brave I might have died. She says I went through a lot of pain.' Her small brow furrowed. 'I don't remember it. Aunt Liz thinks that's the reason I hardly ever cry when I hurt myself. You know, like 'cause I got used to pain as a baby, I'm con... conda...'

'Conditioned to it?' Craig heard his voice as a strangled gasp.

'Yeah!' Melanie beamed at him. 'That's what she said when I jammed my finger in her car door and I didn't even cry a bit! *Not at all.*' She paused and tilted her head to one side, then settled her two tiny hands on his shoulders. 'Do you think I'm brave, Daddy?'

Her face was more hopefully expectant than he'd ever seen it and it rocked him with the force of an earthquake. He nodded, cupping her soft, innocent face in his large hand as he swallowed hard.

'Yeah, sweetheart,' he rasped, 'I think you're brave. Incredibly brave, beautiful and smart.'

Perfect tiny teeth appeared from behind a satisfied grin. 'Were you brave when you got hit with the bat?'

Of their own accord, Craig's arms pulled her small body against his. 'No, honey,' he said, 'I don't think I've ever been brave.'

Only pride stopped him from admitting he was the biggest and most stupid coward God ever put breath into.

CHAPTER ELEVEN

TAYLOR blew a final kiss to her sleeping daughter, then stepped into the upstairs hall sighing with relief at having survived another day under the same roof as Craig. Today was Tuesday, Friday would make three weeks in the cast, then there were only ten days to go. Ugh! Counting days made it seem eternal!

'Taylor?'

She mentally braced herself before turning towards the male voice, but she wasn't prepared for the sight of him, clad only in jeans and towelling his wet hair. Her breath snagged in her throat as her eyes zeroed in on the tanned, muscled expanse of chest on display. The urge to run her fingers through the smattering of dark hair shadowing down over his hard, trim abdomen into a waistband of faded denim made her hands itch so badly that self-preservation demanded her white-knuckled grip on the crutches.

Fighting to rein in her wayward thoughts and get her heart rate back to normal, she averted her eyes, schooling her face to neutrality.

'I want to talk to you before you go to bed. Or—' he draped the towel around his neck and clutched the ends '—should I say *barricade* yourself in your room?'

'I don't know what you're talking about...'

He twisted his mouth in disbelief. 'You know all right, but we'll discuss it further downstairs, after I get dressed.'

The assumption that she'd ask *how high*? when he said *jump* galled her! If he hadn't got the message that she was letting him stay under sufferance, it was time he did!

'By all means, Craig,' she said sweetly. 'But don't be too surprised when you get downstairs and *I'm* not there!'

'Honey,' he drawled, 'it takes me less than a minute to tug a shirt on. Unless you're a lot faster on those things than you look, you can't escape me. You'll hear what I have to say *face to face*, even if I have to knock your bedroom door down to do it.'

His stance, tone and the knowledge of just how determined he could be told her he wasn't joking, but though, as an eighteen-year-old débutante, she may have been fascinated by his street-tough attitude, it hadn't intimidated her. Not then and certainly not now!

'Get this straight, Craig!' she said. 'This is *my* house—'

'Real estate ownership isn't the issue, Taylor.' His pause was the drop-the-shoes-one-at-a-time sort. '*Parenthood* is.'

'Then it'll be a very one-sided conversation, since *your* knowledge is so limited!'

'Maybe,' he said. 'But *your* behaviour the past week hasn't been indicative of someone with five years' head start on me!'

'What's *that* supposed to mean?'

'Meet me in the family room and find out. That way there'll be less chance of your waking Melanie.'

She'd forgotten about Melanie sleeping only metres away and it irked her that *he* hadn't! Her voice dropped to a defiant whisper. 'Fine! But I don't have time to wait all night for you,' she said.

One side of his mouth lifted in cynical amusement. 'Planning a jog around the block, are you?'

She was seated in an armchair, mentally rehearsing how she intended the impending debate to go, when he walked in and quickly snatched up both crutches.

'What the—?'

'For your own safety,' he told her, depositing them on the other side of the room by the fireplace. 'In case you get all steamed up at what I'm going to say and hurt yourself trying to storm from the room.'

'More like for *your* safety, so I don't smack you over the head with them,' she said.

He grinned. 'That, too.'

The male appreciation that lit his eyes as he studied the skimpy black stretch tank top she wore was, Taylor was certain, designed to unnerve her. And if experiencing wavelets of desire in the pit of one's belly was indicative of being *unnerved*, then Craig's tactic was a success. Not that he'd ever know! She folded her arms across her breasts in an action intended to convey she was impatient for him to get to the point of whatever he wanted to discuss; that the action also concealed her breasts' traitorous response to him was an added bonus.

'Are you going to actually *tell* me why you wanted to speak to me or am I expected to read your mind?'

'Tay—' his voice was barely above a whisper '—believe me, if you could read my mind you'd be breathing a lot harder and faster than you are now.'

'That's it!' She pushed herself halfway from the chair, then swore when she realized she couldn't go anywhere.

Grinning like the proverbial Cheshire, Craig strolled to the bar. 'See? I told you I was protecting you from yourself! Drink?'

'No, just a glass. That way I won't stain the carpet when I throw it at you!'

Laughing, he reached for a bottle of bourbon and two tumblers. There was no need for her to tell him what she wanted; six years of marriage meant some things didn't need to be said, but the past few days had created plenty that did. Opening a bottle of Coke, he added it to one of the glasses.

After handing the mixed drink to her, he retreated to a safe distance, where the light scent of her perfume wasn't so distracting. He took a stalling swallow from his own glass as he surveyed the timber-panelled room; the Scandinavian styling of the house was not what he'd have expected to appeal to Taylor. As if reading his mind, her voice broke the silence.

'I haven't got around to redecorating yet. Most of my furniture's still in storage.'

'You've still got this God-awful thing, though,' he said, motioning to the two-metre-by-two-metre handmade rug hanging on the wall. A grotesque, abstract mix of pinks, purples and reds, it had been a wedding present from her parents. He'd never seen any artistic merit in it and believed it had been a subtle reminder to him that he was only a two-bit motor mechanic who was light years away from appreciating the finer things in life even if he had married into one of society's most respected families.

'I keep it,' Taylor was saying, 'because it was one of the few things my parents ever gave me that didn't seem like an apology for not spending enough time with me.'

'So are you going to commission one just like it for Melanie?'

His question bamboozled her. 'Pardon me?'

'I want to know if you're going to give one to Mel to compensate for the fact you aren't spending any time with her these days.'

Not fooled by his offhanded tone, she was instantly on the defensive. 'What the hell are you trying to say?'

'I'm saying that ever since I got here you've been punishing Melanie for spending time with me by avoiding her!'

'That's a lie! I'm not avoiding Mel—'

'No,' he said sagely, 'you're avoiding *me*. But it's Mel who's suffering. Giving her one parent at the expense of another isn't what I call being fair to a kid, Taylor.'

The accusation made her reel, but the blush of guilt warming her face made a denial pointless. Because of the tension in the house when she and Craig were in the same room, she'd gone to pains to stop the situation from arising. For one thing, she'd abandoned breakfast altogether simply to avoid facing him across the table each morning, although for Melanie's sake, she'd forced herself to continue to endure the evening meal with him. Other than that, she'd made sure any contact with Craig was accidental and fleetingly short. She'd even altered well-established daily routines, such as transferring the afternoon snack and the how-was-school chat she shared with Melanie from the kitchen to her bedroom. A ploy, which, while effectively excluding Craig, had in hindsight hardly been subtle or fair.

Taylor had come to regard her temporary sleeping quarters as a *sanctuary*, her only truly safe haven when Craig was in the house, and she retreated there more and more in an attempt to back away from all but the most unavoidable exposure to him. The knowledge that her actions were inadvertently upsetting Melanie left her sick, and she knew Craig was reading her face not her mind when he continued.

'If you think *you* feel bad, Taylor, imagine how Mel's feeling. She asks us to come and watch her play on the trampoline or watch a video or something, and if I say yes, you refuse. Hell, you won't even give her an answer until you know what mine is going to be!'

Not even the coolness of her drink was able to ease the shame burning at Taylor's throat.

'You honestly think she doesn't notice the way you scamper off to your room the minute I join you both in front of the TV?'

'Has...has she said anything?'

'Not directly. She hasn't had to. Hell, I'm the first to admit I'm no expert in the parenting field, but even I'm intuitive enough to pick up on her confusion. But if you think I'll sacrifice the little time I have left here with her so *you* don't look bad, forget it!' he told her.

'I . . . I didn't realize. I . . .' She stopped, unable to find any acceptable explanation.

How could she have let herself become so wrapped up with her own problems that she didn't recognize she was creating ones for her daughter? It was so similar to what her own parents had done that it terrified her. Numb with guilt, she surrendered her empty glass to him and watched without protest as he poured her a second drink. It wasn't until she had half finished it that she realized what she was doing and hastily lowered the glass.

He gave her a half smile. '*Two* drinks are not going to turn you into a candidate for AA.'

'No. But we both know spirits cloud my thinking.'

'If you'll excuse the observation, I think we've just established it hasn't been too red-hot lately anyway.'

'So it would seem.' Her voice was scratchy. 'I guess it means I'm not going to win the Mother-of-the-Year title this year, either.'

'Not without some heavy-duty damage control,' he returned, his tone indicating he knew exactly what was required.

'Such as?'

'Such as putting aside your pride and your antagonism of me and doing what's right for Melanie.'

She opened her mouth to protest, then quickly shut it. He was right. *Again, dammit*! But as difficult as it was going to be to do, there was no other solution. She nodded.

'Good!'

He sounded so cheerfully triumphant Taylor swung towards him even before she'd formulated the snappy retort his tone provoked. But there was no sign of smugness on his face, so she kept silent.

'Now we've sorted that out,' he said, carrying the crutches over to her, 'I was wondering if you still have those videos of Melanie that the hospital took?' At her nod, he added, 'Do you mind if I have a look at them?'

'Er...no. I...I guess not,' she answered, surprised by the request. 'They're in the cabinet under the VCR. I'll...I'll set them up. I'm not sure they're in date order. Mel sometimes looks at them.' She knew she was babbling, but she couldn't help it.

'Don't bother,' he said, intercepting her as she hobbled towards the entertainment unit. A small smile tinged his features. 'Thanks, but I think I can manage on my own. 'Night, Taylor. I'll see you at breakfast.'

The obvious dismissal wounded her far more than it should have and she retreated to her 'sanctuary' with a sense of being utterly alone and hopelessly lonely. Somewhere in the context of the past hour, her emotions had become blurred; hope and reality, fact and fantasy all ran together. The anger that had bubbled within her since Craig's 'confession' of a week ago gave way to tears when the certainty that everything she'd once felt for him was dead now was challenged by a vague feeling that perhaps it still had a faint pulse.

Craig's telephone call midmorning the next day stunned her so much she kept staring at the cordless phone every few seconds to make sure she wasn't dreaming. While breakfast had been a pleasant enough event, there'd been nothing in his demeanour to hint he was considering making the offer he just had.

'Now I don't want you to feel obligated to say yes,' he was saying when she returned the phone to her ear. 'But you've been complaining of being bored, and since I'm so snowed under with these interviews we might be able to kill two birds with one stone, so to speak. Taylor? Are you still there?'

'Yes...'

'So what do you think?'

'You want me to interview some of the applicants for the half-dozen relieving debtors clerks positions Adams

Relief has available?' she repeated, wanting to be certain she'd not misheard him.

'Right. What do you say?'

'Eh . . . well, I'm not sure. Where would I conduct the interviews?'

'Wherever you think is easiest. Home or here at the office—'

'Not at home!' she said quickly. 'I don't want a lot of strangers tramping through the house.'

'Fair enough. I'll have a temporary office set up for you in the interview room here. It'll probably take you two days or so to get through them all. That isn't a problem, is it?'

'Like I've got a really active lifestyle right now.'

His warm male laugh reached right down into her gut. 'Does that mean I can count on your coming in with me tomorrow morning?'

Excitement started to erode her initial surprise. She had the chance to shed her couch-potato existence and be almost *normal*! She could get out of the house and actually *do* something. Something she knew, something she enjoyed.

'Taylor?'

'Tomorrow's fine,' she said. 'Although my cast may not coordinate with my dress-for-success professional wardrobe too well.' Even as she said the words, she was trying to picture what exactly she did have to wear.

'Taylor, you'll be sitting behind a desk. No one will even *see* the bottom half of you!'

His tone, suggesting she was worrying about nothing, was a tad too patronizing for her to ignore. 'Oh, well, in that case,' she said airily, 'I'll just pull on a blouse and snazzy blazer and go naked from the waist down.'

There was a long beat of silence before Craig spoke again. 'Do that, honey, and you'll have *me* pulling off the blouse and snazzy blazer before we even leave the house!'

*   *   *

As offices went, the interview room made a good closet, but Taylor was too satisfied with herself to allow such minor details to bother her.

She'd conducted eleven interviews since arriving in the office at ten and so far had short-listed four applicants to return for a second interview on Monday. She was amazed at how easily all the old instincts for spotting candidates ideal for temporary work resurfaced. While there had been three other applicants with excellent debtors experience, she'd recognized they weren't suited to shifting from one job to another and, after checking with Craig's secretary, referred them to a firm that dealt with finding people permanent positions.

A rap on the door pulled her from her thoughts and an immaculately suited Craig entered before she had a chance to even think the words *come in*. The force of his masculinity as he eased himself onto the corner of her desk shrank the room to claustrophobic proportions. Realizing she was staring at him in a way which might be recognized as the blatant admiration that it was, Taylor scrambled to appear as if her mind was on the job rather than him.

'I've come up with four possible starters,' she said, shoving a buff-coloured manila folder at him. 'If the standard remains constant for this afternoon and tomorrow, I figure there'll be between eight and twelve for final interviews on Monday.'

'Good,' he said, without looking at the contents. 'Ready to call it a day?'

She blinked. 'But it's only a little after twelve.'

'I was told you'd skipped morning tea,' he said, raising a disapproving eyebrow. 'And as a guy from a blue-collar background with an inbred respect for union rules, I'm making myself personally responsible to see you have a decent lunch.'

'Oh, well, thanks.' She grinned. 'Just between you and me, I'm starved.' She reached for the phone on her desk.

'Let me check what time my first afternoon interview is scheduled.'

He leaned across the desk, one long finger depressing the telephone's connection bar. 'It's been rescheduled,' he said, his face less than a foot from hers. 'Until tomorrow.'

'Why?'

'Because by the time we finish lunch, it'll be time to go and collect Mel from school.'

Drowning in his nearness, she sensed rather than physically felt him take the phone from her hand. 'But...but she doesn't finish till three. That's two and a half hours away.'

'Allow,' he said, a hand grazing the side of her neck, 'an hour for lunch...' His head was drawing perceptibly near. 'And another forty-five minutes to drive to the school...'

Taylor's brain told her to move, but her body didn't cooperate; her gaze was transfixed on the male face and lips drawing closer and closer to hers. Bit by bit her vision of the room's peach walls was reduced while her appreciation of his sexuality increased. Her heart rate was picking up, too, getting faster and faster as Craig's mouth drew nearer and nearer....

'But...but that...' She swallowed hard, desperate to both lengthen and shorten the time before she had to make a conscious effort to stop what Craig was so obviously intent on doing. 'That still leaves um...um...forty-five minutes.'

A slow smile revealed perfect white teeth only millimetres from her own.

'Ah, yes, Tay.' His thumb grazed the shape of her mouth. 'But you haven't allowed for the most obvious thing.'

'Wh-what's that?'

'The fact you're incredibly beautiful, and that I need to spend time tasting that beauty.' A shiver skipped along her spine as his bottom lip brushed over hers, butterfly soft. 'But it's up to you,' he said, letting his tongue touch the corner of her mouth. 'What do you want to do with the spare forty-five minutes?'

On a shivery sigh, she wrapped her arms around his neck and let action be her response. . . .

CHAPTER TWELVE

AT THE first taste of her, with both bliss and dread racing through him, Craig knew he was certifiably insane. Never had surrender to passion been more ill-advised or destined to end unfulfilled; never before had he experienced the sense of risk, of *danger*. But he deepened the kiss, knowing the danger had nothing to do with the unlocked door and the chance that any second someone might walk through it. This was an emotional peril he courted.

Once he'd been as sure of Taylor as he was that night followed day; now, as her mouth suckled his, he wasn't even sufficiently confident to stop long enough to find a more comfortable position, for fear she'd remember all the reasons she didn't want to be doing this.

But he didn't just *want* this; he needed it! He needed Taylor more than his own heart, but in one week, *only seven lousy days*, she'd be back on her own two feet and demanding he exit her life! The sudden ache of despair the thought prompted intensified his desire to absorb everything currently available to him. To touch and taste as much of her as he could in as little time as possible, before she pulled away from his touch...and his life.

Taylor's entire being reeled under the urgency and fervour driving Craig's exploration of her mouth. Every pulse point in her body switched from normal to full speed the instant he'd invaded her lips; her mind shut down everything bar the deliciously male flavour of him. His hands sliding down the sensitized skin of her neck and caressing her silk-covered breasts incited a feral arousal, which instinctively spurred her to arch into his hold. In the dim recesses of her mind, she was aware of one hand struggling with buttons as the other massaged the fullness of her breasts and she cursed the clothing delaying intimate contact with her flesh. Yet just when she was sure she'd explode from the burning frustration budding in her nipples, her bra was shoved aside and blissful relief delivered by the pressure of hot male fingers. A coil of erotic delight radiating from his touch tugged at the very core of her and made her stomach muscles contract; her heartfelt groan was absorbed in his kiss and reached her ears as nothing more than a tiny, satisfied purr.

The touch of his palm against her ribcage electrified her blood and activated a hungry need to get closer— closer to the solid, warm heat of him. Closer to herself. She half rose from her chair, bracing her arms on the desk while her tongue duelled frantically with his, alternating between the recesses of her mouth and his. She was drunk with the taste of him, high on his touch, but greedily she sought more, their oral feast inciting rather than appeasing her hunger. When anxious male fingers tugged her blouse from the waistband of her skirt, the anticipation of what would follow turned her arms to jelly and she slumped down into her chair. The sudden absence of his touch drew a startled gasp from her.

Physically shaking and struggling for much-needed oxygen, Taylor closed her eyes and tried to compose herself. A million different thoughts were crowding her passion-drugged brain, but one stood way above the mental mêlée. *She loved this man*. Not in a civilized, safe, till-death-us-do-part way, but in a through-all-eternity way. Craig Adams was the other half of her soul. Always had been; always would be. The knowledge hit her with the force of a blow, yet came as no surprise.

She'd sensed it at eighteen and followed her instincts with the unquestioning trust that belongs only to the young. Five years ago, she'd begun to fear and doubt the obsessive need she felt for Craig and she'd run from it, twistedly believing the strength of her love for him would limit the amount she had to give Melanie.

But she'd been wrong. Totally and utterly wrong. *Unjustly* wrong! She'd been afraid of the exact same thing she'd ridiculed Craig for—believing parental love encroached on the strength of true love. *Now* she understood the love she felt for Craig was so elemental to her existence that it was the basis of whatever love she gave to others. Melanie. Liz. *Anyone*! Indeed, it wasn't until she'd met Craig and had experienced the warmth of his love that she'd been able to establish a worthwhile relationship with her parents.

She tried to analyse where this startling insight left her and the implications it would have on the future. Or, more importantly, on the *present*! Her eyes flew open and she stared at Craig; brown eyes, pupils dilated by passion, returned her gaze, his uneven breathing matching her own.

Searching his face, she tried to ascertain if the kiss had affected him as profoundly as it had her. Not in the physical sense, but in the *spiritual*. Had it stirred him only on a sexual level or had it reached beyond and touched him soul deep?

'Look,' he said, moving awkwardly from the desk and regaining his feet. 'Let's not analyse this thing to death. It was bound to happen and we both know it. Let's not make a big deal out of it.'

Not make a big deal out of it? How could she *not*? Her very perceptions of life had been picked up, shaken and turned on their ear! She felt like she'd been struck by lightning and the wisdom of Solomon at the same time! Yet it was apparent that Craig, who was reefing at his tie as if trying to choke himself, *had not*!

Taylor knew that until she had time to sit down and decide how best to deal with the changes her new insight was bound to create, there was no point going off half-

cocked. She bit down on the smile sparked by her un-
intentional mental pun and, forcing a calmness she was
light years from feeling, started to button her blouse.

'I'm not going to make a big deal out of it, Craig.'
She smiled. 'Now where did you say we were having
lunch?'

Two things registered with Taylor the instant she awoke
Saturday morning. The first was that sleep *had* been
bestowed on her at some stage in the pre-dawn hours;
the other was that Melanie was outside her bedroom door
alternately giggling and making shushing noises at the
top of her voice.

Flicking her gaze at the digital clock, she only had
time to frown at the 10:47 it indicated, before the door
was pushed open and Uncle Bernie bounded through it.
The bed springs compressed under the dog's huge weight
at the same time that Melanie announced, 'See, Daddy?
I told you she was awake!'

Taylor blinked as her daughter, copying Bernie's actions, tested the mattress's durability further. 'We're
going to the zoo! Daddy said so.'

'I *suggested* it,' Craig qualified. 'If it was all right by
you.'

He stood braced in the doorway, a half smile playing
on his face as his eyes flicked over the copious quantity
of skin Taylor's negligée exposed. Feeling her face heat,
Taylor drew the sheet higher. Though Thursday had
given her a new perspective on her feelings for him, she
still couldn't guess at his.

Yesterday at the office she'd found her heart leaping
every time there was a knock at the door until she'd
learned Craig was out at a meeting. When he'd returned, she'd noticed a subtle reticence in his demeanour. She equated it with the kind of subdued
reluctance one expected to see in a man who knew he

had no choice but to swim across a crocodile-infested river, yet didn't want to admit it.

She smiled as much at the bizarre nature of her thoughts as at him. 'Mel will love it. She's been dying to go—'

'You're coming, too, Mummy!'

'Uh, I don't think so,' Taylor said, wishing otherwise. 'I'm in no shape to go tramping round Taronga Park—'

'We could hire you a wheelchair.' The tone of Craig's voice was no indication of whether he was simply being polite or genuinely hoping for her company.

'Yeah! Me and Daddy could take turns pushing you! Oh, please, Mummy? *Please.*'

Taylor sighed through a smile at her daughter's clasped-hand entreaty.

'Listen, Mel, how about you give your mother time to think about it while we fix her a pot of coffee?'

Taylor directed a grateful look at Craig. 'Good idea!' She grinned and dropped a quick kiss on her daughter's cheek, simultaneously patting her bottom. 'Scoot and let me get dressed while I make up my mind.'

'OK.' The child scampered off the bed, dog in pursuit. 'But you *have* to come! You simply *have* to come.'

The moment the door closed behind them, Taylor rolled off the bed. She *did* have to go. Her heart demanded it.

'Get me a saw!'

Craig grinned as Taylor directed the demand to the huge hound slobbering over her at the foot of the stairs. Satisfied Melanie was too bone tired to be waked by an atom bomb much less the loud complaints of her mother, he started down the stairs.

'What happened?'

Taylor's head jerked round. 'I'm sitting at the bottom of the stairs on my backside and you have to *ask*? What are you, a slow learner?'

He raised a mocking eyebrow. 'Three weeks on those things and you're calling *me* a slow learner?'

'Oh, shut up!' she told him, hauling herself upright with the aid of the banister. 'And get that stupid grin off your face!'

'Is that any way to speak to a man who's devoted his entire day to taking care of you?'

'Well, it was your bright idea to go to the zoo!' Immediately following her words, contrition crossed her features. 'Sorry, that was unfair. I'm taking my frustration out on you.'

Craig looked down at how the Indian cotton dress she wore fell in soft, almost transparent folds from its tied shoulders and only wished she was talking about the same frustration that afflicted *him*.

'Go sit down and I'll fix us a drink,' he said. 'You're probably feeling the exhaustion of the day more than I am.'

'Yeah, right,' she agreed. 'After all, I had to sit in a wheelchair and be pushed everywhere, while *you* only had to go on every kid's ride available, walk from one end of Taronga Park to the other—often piggybacking a five-year-old—and then carry said five-year-old all the way to the car.' She grinned. 'I'm far more entitled to be exhausted than you!'

Her smile damn near made his hand tremble as he splashed Coke into her drink, though how it could still affect him so strongly when he'd been exposed to it all day puzzled him. He couldn't deny the excursion had depleted his energy level, but one look at Taylor rejuvenated parts of his anatomy that sadly weren't getting the exercise they desired. He handed her her drink, but rather than joining her on the sofa, lowered himself into an armchair; tempting fate wasn't something he was prepared to do right now.

'You think Melanie enjoyed herself?' he asked.

'Are you kidding? She had a ball!'

He frowned. 'She seemed pretty quiet coming home.'

'Craig, she'd literally run herself speechless!' Taylor's face was full of gentle amusement. 'She really— Aaahhhhh!'

He was at her side even before she set her glass aside and grabbed frantically at the cast. 'What's up? What's the matter?'

'Knitting needle!' she muttered through gritted teeth. 'Get me a—' She swore, frantically trying to force her fingers inside the casing on her leg.

With fear clenching his gut, Craig tried to still her hand. 'Honey, take it easy. Just calm—'

'Get me a goddamn knitting needle!' she screamed, slapping his hands away.

'A *knitting needle*?'

Taylor realized he had no idea what her problem was, but now wasn't the time for explanations! 'There's one on the table beside my bed. *Get it*!'

'What—?'

'Just get it, will you? I'm in agony here!'

When he finally returned with the item in question, Taylor immediately snatched it from him and shoved it down her cast.

'What on earth—?'

'The cast,' she managed to say in a sigh of blissful relief. 'It...it's started to itch. The hospital said this would happen.'

His frown was doubtful. 'This is *normal*?'

'Apparently.' She continued to move the needle as far into the cast as she could without losing her grip on it. Starting to feel some relief, she sighed and gave him an apologetic smile. 'Sorry about yelling at you like that, but lord, you have no idea what it's like to have an itch you can't scratch.'

'Don't I?' he asked, cocking one eyebrow.

As her stomach dropped to her toes, she looked away, wishing she knew how to diffuse the sexual tension arching between them or had the guts to do something about it.

'Here,' Craig said, startling her by prying her fingers from the metal needle she was absently rubbing down her leg. 'Lie back and relax for a while.'

The intended protest died as he started to gently work the needle against the skin inside the cast and she let her head sink back against the soft leather sofa. Perhaps it was the mix of a tiring day and the bourbon, but within seconds the tension started to flow from her muscles. Perhaps, she thought, it was simply a case of Craig being the right man to scratch her itch....

The late-afternoon sun was long gone when she opened her eyes and the only source of light came from the kitchen behind her. So, too, did the tempting aroma of fried chicken, and hunger sent her glance in that direction.

'I fell asleep, huh?'

Looking up from the meal he was obviously preparing, Craig nodded. 'Told you you were exhausted.'

Still drowsy, she was unprepared for the impact of his smile and had to wait until her heart stopped ramming her ribcage before she could speak. 'You must be pretty beat yourself. You didn't have to go to the trouble of cooking.'

'I didn't. I rang the local chicken shop and had it delivered.'

'You did? But... but they don't do home delivery.'

'They do if you promise a big enough tip.' He grinned. 'Stay there,' he instructed when she started to move. 'No point using the dining room just for finger food. We might as well eat in the family room and see what's on TV.'

Nostalgia swamped Taylor. It was years since she'd spent a Saturday night eating dinner in front of the television. Eleven years in fact. Not since, when newly married and determined to survive without assistance from her parents, she and Craig had been too financially strapped to eat out or party. Then as their business had picked up, so had their social life, and there hadn't been time for finger food and television. It was, Taylor thought, a prime example of the saying 'You don't know what you've got till it's gone'.

Craig dragged the coffee-table close to the sofa, then tossed the remote and viewing guide into her lap. 'Check out what's on offer while I bring in dinner.'

'What do you prefer?' she called out. 'A detective show followed by a comedy talk show, a documentary on the development of the helicopter, reruns of a couple of bland sitcoms or a Spanish film with English and French subtitles?'

'Aren't there any *decent* movies on?' he asked, setting down a plate of fried chicken, another of hot chips and a bottle of wine.

There was, but as a concession to her overstressed hormones, Taylor didn't think it would be a good idea to watch it with *him*. 'Uh, yeah, but you've probably seen it.' At his questioning glance, she cleared her throat and gave her attention to the chicken. '*When Harry Met Sally* with Meg Ryan and—'

'The doco on helicopters sounds good,' he said.

His silence during the next twenty or so minutes had Taylor wishing he'd opted for the movie. At least the movie would have come with commercial breaks, thus providing an opportunity where he *might* have spoken to her. Obviously the advancements in rotor technology were far more engrossing than her company! So far, apart from a request that she turn the volume up and two enquiries as to whether she wanted more wine, he hadn't said a word. Nor for that matter even glanced up from his position on the floor to where she was stretched out with both legs up on the sofa. She on the other hand had been so aware of his elbow occasionally brushing against the knee of her good leg that she was all but oblivious to anything the dull-voiced narrator was saying.

'Gee, *that* was fascinating,' she said when the credits finally started to roll. 'But with all due respect, *I'm* going to choose what we watch next!'

His profile hinted at a muscle twitching near his mouth. 'No problem,' he said, getting to his feet and stacking the empty plates. 'I think I'll call it a day.'

Disappointment crushed her. 'But it's only nine-thirty!'

'Yeah, but Mel dragged me out of bed before dawn this morning and I suspect she will tomorrow, too,' he finished drily.

'Oh, I'm sorry. I'll speak with her about—'

'No! Don't.' His smile was understandingly gentle. 'I wasn't complaining. Truth is, I'd stay up around the clock if she wanted.'

She followed him with her gaze as he crossed to the kitchen, wishing he'd change his mind and elect to stay and talk with her. But as her eyes honed in on the fluid movement of muscles beneath his snug jeans, she was honest enough to admit her craving went beyond mere conversation. Stifling a groan, she drained her wineglass and switched off the television.

'Changed your mind?' he asked, returning to the family room.

Not trusting herself to look at him, she nodded. 'I think I'll read in bed for a while.' She levered herself onto her feet and was reaching for the crutches when his hand stilled her arm. His fingers against her bare skin sent heat spiralling through her and she knew her face was flushed when she lifted it questioningly to him.

'Could we talk for a moment? There's something I want to say.'

Again her heart started thumping fit to explode and she was hard-pressed to do more than nod. Certain her bones were dissolving as a result of his tender gaze, she sank back onto the sofa. She expected, or perhaps *hoped* was a more accurate word, that he would join her, but he didn't. Instead, he stood looking down at her as if trying to second-guess what she was thinking. On the off chance he could, Taylor filled her mind with thoughts of her love for him, but the longer his silence continued the more she lost faith in mental telepathy.

'So what was it you wanted to say, Craig?' she prompted when her nerves could stand no more.

He blinked and shook his head as if coming out of a trance, then crouched down and reached out to cup her cheek. Her pulse went back into overdrive.

'I want to apologize for not believing you when you said you didn't deliberately get pregnant. Given the way my parents manipulated me as a kid, trust has never been one of my strong suits, but for what it's worth...' He sighed, his thumb grazing her jaw. 'I do believe you.'

Taylor could barely breathe. *He believed her*! *Finally he believed her*! All she'd ever wanted was his trust and his love and now she had them! Happiness was saturating her to the point where she thought she'd drown in it. Tempted to throw herself into his arms, she held back, wanting to hear him declare his love. Wanting him to admit that Thursday in the office *had* been a big deal because, like her, he'd felt the truth, the depth and the rightness of their love. Sure, it might have taken him a few extra days to recognize the importance of what they'd shared that day, but, she mused with a grin, as Liz had often told her, men were slower on the uptake in most things!

'What...what made you change your mind?' she asked, even though she knew the answer.

'Logic.'

Wrong answer!

She stared at him in wholesale disbelief. '*Logic?*'

His hand abandoned her face to rake through his hair. 'Taylor, if you'd ever been selfish enough to disregard my feelings about children and deliberately try to get pregnant, you'd hardly give me the opportunity to be a part of Melanie's life now.' An ironic twist tugged at his mouth. 'Plus you'd have spent the past few years poisoning her mind so that she'd hate me. *Not*,' he said, 'telling her things like "some mummies and daddies live apart because it makes them better parents".'

Taylor closed her eyes, her mind and senses spinning sickeningly out of control; despair choked the life from the vibrant hope that moments ago danced within her. Lifting her lashes, she saw he was now standing by the fireplace, but in her heart she knew the distance between them was far greater.

'You and Mel have obviously done some heavy-duty talking,' she said, saying aloud what had been only a thought.

'Yeah, we have.' His expression was one of a man who could hardly believe his good fortune. 'I'll never be able to thank you enough for giving me an opportunity I didn't deserve. Having this time with Mel has meant more to me than you'll ever know.'

What she heard in his voice cut her to the quick. His departure was imminent; in six days he'd be gone. Fighting to be sensible about something her heart could make no sense of, she forced herself to speak.

'She's going to miss having you around all the time.' *So am I*, she screamed silently.

'Not half as much as I'll miss her.' Something in the tone of his admission drew her eyes to his. 'I love her, Taylor,' he said. 'I don't know when or how it happened, but I do love her. I don't expect you to believe it. I don't quite believe it myself. I never expected it to happen.' He gave a boyishly bemused smile. 'Guess she just kind of snuck in under my guard.'

Taylor couldn't speak past the lump in her throat, but as tears trickled silently down her cheeks, she realized that it didn't matter because she couldn't think of anything to say anyway. She couldn't *think* at all.

'Would I be asking too much,' he continued, 'if I said I'd like to see her on a weekly basis and maybe have her spend one entire weekend a month with me? More if you don't mind. Maybe I could have her when you've got basketball or... or something.'

The requests came with enthusiastic rapidity. Twice Taylor opened her mouth to respond, only to shut it again as emotional confusion numbed her brain. Physically, though, the pain slashing through her was so brutal she half expected to find herself sitting in a pool of her own blood.

'At least think about it over the next few days,' he urged when she remained silent. 'I won't make any promises to Melanie until you decide. And I'll trust your judgement,' he hastily assured her. 'It's your call on timetables and time limits. I'll work in with anything you want.'

Taylor didn't know *what* she wanted any more! But suddenly love without trust seemed like a much better deal than *trust without love*.

CHAPTER THIRTEEN

'WATCH, Daddy!'

Craig did as his daughter commanded, duly applauding when she executed a simple tumble on her trampoline.

Face flushed, she pushed a curtain of hair from her eyes and grinned at him. 'Soon I'll be able to do them in the air!'

'I don't doubt it!' His smile came from the simple joy of his daughter's own pleasure. 'But just so you don't break any limbs, promise me you won't try it unless an adult's watching you. Right?' The only response forthcoming was continued bouncing. '*Right*, Melanie?' he repeated.

'Aww. OK.'

Satisfied with the grudging agreement, he turned his attention to the patio, where Taylor lay stretched out on a sun lounge reading. He wasn't fooled. The book was simply another means of avoiding speaking with him— the least creative in a long line of tactics she'd employed since Saturday night.

Sunday morning, she'd had him wash the car and the dog, the latter a particularly wet and exhausting task, before producing a grocery list she 'urgently' needed filled. He was definitely slow, Craig decided, because even after spending the better part of the afternoon shopping for enough food to feed the entire Australian army for a year, he hadn't started to suspect Taylor's motives until that night when, claiming a headache, she retreated to her bedroom right after dinner.

His intention to confront her over her attitude at breakfast Monday morning faltered at the sight of her eyes, red-rimmed and puffy with dark shadows beneath them. She'd looked so genuinely ill he'd felt like a jerk for questioning her behaviour—a worried jerk. However, when he'd phoned during the day to see how she was feeling, her terse response made it clear it wasn't her health that was bothering her, but *him*. His presence and the fact he wanted access to Melanie. She didn't trust him with her daughter; didn't trust him not to disappoint the little girl as he'd so obviously disappointed her.

The knowledge was like a knife twisting in his gut. Again he cursed himself for not waiting until Friday to raise the matter of his role in Melanie's future. At least then he might've been able to enjoy a few more days of the fantasy-like happiness the three of them had shared together at the zoo. Yet instead of being grateful for the status quo, he'd gone rushing ahead, trying to deal with problems that hadn't even arisen and remembering too late the advice he'd received as an apprentice mechanic: 'Don't go fiddlin' about with an engine's timing if the car's already runnin' smooth!' In other words, *If it ain't broke, don't fix it*!

Good advice, he acknowledged in hindsight, but now, thanks to him, things *were* 'broke' and he had to start making some repairs before Taylor's cast came off in three days' time. Already he felt the ache of missing her; was desperate for the sound of her voice, the warmth of her smile. Muttering a curse, he strode towards the patio.

'Decided what you want me to put on for dinner?' he asked, lowering himself into the chair next to hers.

When she shook her head without looking up, he fought the impulse to rip the book from her hands and hurl it across the yard, not sure if his irritation stemmed from her disinterest or his own frustration. He'd known from the word go his time here would end the moment Taylor was fully mobile again, but until the trip to the zoo, he hadn't understood what he would be leaving behind. That one day had been enough to make him realize what he'd wanted from life in the past *wasn't* what he wanted any more; had started him thinking, *and believing*, that given time perhaps they could be a family.

He wasn't foolish enough to think Taylor wouldn't want him to leave at the end of the week, but he'd hoped their joint interest in Melanie would keep them in close contact and give him time to win back Tay's love and respect. The truth was that he wanted, *needed*, to be a part of *her* life every bit as much as he did their daughter's. Even if he could never be her lover again, a thought that caused him more pain than he could have imagined possible, he needed to maintain personal interaction with her on some level.

The admission brought him face to face with the idea that had been running through his head for over a week. An idea he'd hoped would also occur to Taylor and that she'd be the one to voice it. So far he'd waited in vain. Whether it was because she hadn't even considered the possibility or because she wasn't interested, he didn't know, but the only way to find out was to come right out and ask.

The grim line of her mouth as she practically glared at the book made him mentally pause. No, perhaps a less direct approach might get a more positive response....

'You, eh, didn't ask how the final interviews went yesterday,' he said, keeping his voice deliberately lazy.

No reaction.

He tried again. 'I made my final decision today.'

For a second, Taylor considered remaining mute, then changed her mind. It wasn't just childish to try to block out Craig's presence. It was *impossible*! If she couldn't do it when he was at work, she sure couldn't do it when he was sitting only centimetres away and his voice was washing over her like a caress. Yet talking to him meant taking the risk he'd bring up the subject of Melanie spending time with him; this was something she wasn't happy about and consequently felt racked by guilt because she knew she *should* be. After all, wasn't *that* the reason she'd moved back to Sydney? And it was what Melanie desperately wanted....

Conscious of Craig's steady gaze on her, she snapped the book shut and shoved aside the doubts that had been plaguing her by day and keeping her sleepless by night. At least discussing Adams Relief was a safe topic; it didn't involve her emotions.

'I didn't ask,' she said, sparing him only a token glance, 'because, of the twelve applicants I sent to you, six were head and shoulders above the rest.'

'Mmmm. I thought Carruthers and Logan were exceptional—'

'*What*?' She spun her head to face him, unable to believe her ears. '*Carruthers and Logan* were two of your top six choices?'

He frowned. 'You wouldn't have chosen them?'

'No way! I mean they looked good when I interviewed them Thursday, but not when compared to the applicants I saw on Friday.'

'But, Tay, remember you've been out of the business a long time.'

'Not *that* long!' she retorted, resenting the implication that her executive skills had declined. 'And if you thought those two were in the top six, well, all I can say is maybe *you* ought to think about getting out of the business!'

'And leave you to run it, I presume?'

'No! I...I didn't mean *that*!'

He watched her through half-closed eyes, his smile patronizing. 'OK, I believe you. So what six would you have picked?'

'Sinclair, Reid, Barossi,' she said quickly, ticking them off on her fingers. 'The tall, skinny guy...I can't think of his name—'

'Curtis,' Craig supplied.

'Yeah, him.' She racked her brains for the names of the remaining two applicants she'd considered certainties. 'Oh, yeah! And that Angela Davis and the woman who used to work for the temping firm in New Zealand...I think her name was Sutherland.'

'*Sunder*land,' he corrected, linking his fingers behind his head and reclining on his lounger. He sent her a probing look. 'They're your six? Curtis, Sinclair, Reid, Davis, Barossi and Sunderland.'

She nodded. He said nothing, his face unreadable. 'Well?' she prodded. 'How do they differ from your choices.'

'They don't.'

'But you said you hired Carruthers—'

'Nope!' he interrupted, shaking his head. 'You jumped to that assumption all by yourself.' The glint in his brown eyes matched his devilish grin.

She sent him a lethal look. 'Which is what you intended.'

He shrugged. 'Just wanted to see if you were as confident in your judgement as you used to be.'

'Why?'

'Because I'd like you to think about resuming your position with the company.'

To say she was stunned would have been a major understatement. He had to be crazy! He must think *she* was crazy to have asked her!

She stared at him. 'You're joking, right?'

'No, Taylor. I'm serious. It makes perfect sense.'

He sat up, then swung around to face her earnestly, his arms resting on his knees. Since arriving home with Mel, he'd changed from his business suit into cut-off jeans and a black T-shirt, but Taylor knew that while she might be distracted by the smooth corded muscles of his arms and legs, when it came to the business, Craig's mind never slipped from three-piece-suit mode.

'Look,' he said, intruding on her silent admiration of his thighs, '*you* want a job, and I'm going to have to reduce my workload if I'm to have more time to spend with Melanie. So—'

'I haven't decided on a timetable or anything else yet!' she told him quickly. 'I'm not ready to make definite plans about that.'

His face tensed with hostility, and she was bracing herself for an argument on her procrastination when he sighed, his entire body once again relaxed.

'OK, fine. I understand that. I'm not trying to pressure you. But the fact remains, Taylor, you want a job. And since you're half owner of Adams Relief, it makes sense for you to be involved in the business. Plus you could make your hours as flexible as they need to be to fit in with Melanie's school.'

'I'm only looking to work part-time anyway,' she said. 'I've no intention of taking a job that *doesn't* slot in with school hours.'

'Ah, yes!' He latched onto her words like a pit bull onto steak. 'But what about school vacations? I doubt you'll find an employer willing to give you time off during *all* the school holidays!'

Craig sensed he'd hit on something she hadn't considered when her eyes widened and the outright refusal in them faded. He hoped it was enough to sell her on the idea. The hesitant look she sent him and the way her teeth continued to worry her bottom lip hinted it wasn't and that *he* was the negative factor in the equation.

'Look, Tay, it'll be strictly business all the way. If you're concerned I'll step out of line like I did the other day, *don't be.*'

His words weren't the reassurance he intended because what worried Taylor about 'the other day' was that it was becoming more and more apparent that while it had meant *nothing* to him it meant *everything* to her!

'It's the ideal solution, Taylor. For you, me *and* for Melanie.'

Taylor bit her lip. On the surface it might look that way, but could she, feeling as she did, share an office with him and not be haunted by the memories of the illicit lovemaking they'd shared there in the past? In practical terms the offer was tempting, but in emotional terms it was suicidal! Never in a million years had she imagined Craig would entertain such a notion. Not even when he'd asked her to help out last week. And since then she'd been too preoccupied trying to work through feelings she couldn't even begin to understand! How could she love Craig, *want* him to love Melanie, yet feel resentful about sharing her daughter with him? How could she want to keep father and daughter apart when she knew Melanie adored him?

Oh, God! She was so confused! And it seemed like every time she drew breath, Craig was waiting to complicate her mind or her heart—or both. Maybe when the cast came off and he moved back to his apartment, she'd be able to breathe easily and think clearly again. At the very least she needed to *think*! Right now her brain was in such a state of turmoil she couldn't give him a decision on something as mundane as what she wanted for dinner, let alone a matter of this magnitude! An immediate yes or no could have disastrous consequences.

If working with Craig was going to keep her under this much emotional pressure, all the holidays in the world wouldn't matter. But if *not* seeing him was going to have the same results... Her gaze darted to where Melanie was now playing ball with Uncle Bernie and one thing became crystal clear. Whatever answer she gave, she had to be *certain* it was the right one. Because she knew she'd be useless as a mother if she remained as emotionally screwed up as she was now.

'Can I think about it for a few days?' she asked softly.
'Sure,' he said, getting to his feet. 'There's no rush.'

Craig entered the house braced for the enthusiastic
greeting he'd come to expect from Uncle Bernie each
afternoon. It reminded him of the way Dino flattened
Fred Flintstone when he arrived home from work
although, unlike Fred, Craig had so far managed not to
end up flat on his back. He also knew it was the tiny
form of Mel, following him into the house, the dog was
most eager to see. Obligingly he stepped aside to no
longer impede the reunion between the two.

'Hi, Mummy! I'm home,' Melanie announced in a
singsong tone, charging towards the rear of the house
with the dog at her heels.

Following in the wake of the child and dog, Craig
smiled at Taylor's equally musical response of 'Hi,
sweetheart! I guessed.'

Melanie dropped her bag and school beret in the
middle of the room *en route* to kiss her mother. Craig
ached to do the same. Taylor's beautiful face was bright
with pleasure, the smile she bestowed on her daughter
warmer than any he'd seen on her face in days. She was
standing at the breakfast bar in a long emerald dress
that gave added life to her eyes, yet it wasn't simply the
effect of her clothing that made her seem so... so *alive*.
It was something else. Something else had happened to—

The cast!

His gaze darted to the long, gauzy folds of the dress,
but the bulk of the plaster was still evident; relief set his
heart back to its normal rate. For a fearful second, he'd
thought she'd had it removed a day early. He drew a
deep, grateful breath; even a mere twenty-four hours
more here was better than leaving tonight.

'Wow, chocolate cake!' Melanie exclaimed. 'Did you
make it?'

'No, Liz popped in this afternoon with it,' Taylor said, slicing the layered cream concoction.

'Can I have some?'

'You can have some after you take off your school uniform.'

With a delighted cheer, the child ran from the room, snatching up bag and beret as she went.

'What about me?' Craig asked, setting aside his attaché case and reefing at his tie. 'Do I have to take my clothes off, too, before I can have some? Because I'd be only too happy to oblige.'

A flash of heat lit Taylor's eyes, but it was gone before he could feel its warmth.

'That won't be necessary. I'm sure you can manage to eat it without getting it all over yourself.' She slid a generous wedge onto a plate and held it out to him. 'I've made a pot of tea, but you'll have to pour it.'

'Thanks, but I'll have a cold drink instead.' Aware of the disapproving way she was looking at him as he moved to the refrigerator, he added, '*Do you mind*?'

'If you have a cold drink, no. If you strip in my kitchen, yes.'

Taylor was thankful that his comprehension skills kicked in before his fast-moving fingers released any more of his shirt buttons! But then, as if it hadn't been hot enough *before* the top four had parted company to display a vee of tanned flesh, he proceeded to take a can of Coke from the refrigerator and roll it over his face and neck! The blatant sexuality of the action was enough to make her feel faint.

'Ahhh!' he sighed. 'That's better. Lord, it's hot!'

'Tell me about it,' she muttered, wishing only climatic heat responsible for the increase in *her* body temperature!

'Is it my imagination or is it hotter in here than it is outside?'

'I'd *love* to say it's your imagination,' she said drily. 'But unfortunately the air-conditioning packed in this morning.' *Not that* you're *helping things any*! she silently added.

'Have you called a repairman?'

She rolled her eyes. 'Heavens! Why didn't I think of that? Silly me only thought to call about *fifteen* different repairmen.'

He reached past her, helping himself to another slab of cake. She held her breath as a defence against the sensations his hip created as it brushed against hers.

'I take it you had no luck.'

Her mind was slow to register he was still talking about repairmen. She gave herself a mental shake, pleased Mel had reappeared.

'Actually,' she said, taking the school memos the child thrust at her, 'one guy told me I was in luck. He can get here Monday.'

'We'll melt before then,' Craig muttered. 'I'll get changed and take a look at it now.'

Taylor stopped her perusal of the school newsletter. 'Don't be silly! I don't expect you to do that.'

'Do you really want to put up with this heat until Monday?'

'No, but—'

'Then I'll take a look at it.'

'But... but it's too hot...' A droll twist contorted his mouth. 'You know what I mean! Why go up in the roof when you don't have to?'

'Because I won't be able to stand this for another three days.'

'You're leaving tomor—' Her words stopped as a cold chill seeped into her body. Craig, too, stiffened, his glance shifting to the family room, where Melanie was watching television. In the ensuing uneasy silence, the only indication of his emotions was the effortless ease with which his hand crushed the empty drink can.

'Taylor,' he said wearily, 'give it up, OK?'

'Fine. But do you *know* anything about air-conditioning systems?'

'When you first met me, I was a mechanic, remember?'

'You were a *motor* mechanic!'

'That's right . . . and air-conditioners,' he said slowly as if she were a two-year-old, 'have motors.'

'Oh, I give up!' she said, tossing the school notices in the air. 'You might not have grease under your finger-nails any more, Craig Adams, but it's obviously still in your blood.'

Stepping closer, he brushed his knuckles along her cheek. 'There're a lot of things still in my blood.'

Immobilized by his touch and hypnotized by the thick-lashed brown eyes holding her own captive, Taylor could do nothing but look up into his handsome face. Yet the remoteness of Craig's questioning expression made her realize *his* gaze was directed inward, rather than at her. What was it he was asking himself? Was he, like her, trying to gauge the wisdom of taking the one small step needed to bring them chest to chest? Were his thoughts making his heart thump as violently as hers, so loudly that it drowned out all other sound?

Her eyes went to his partially exposed skin. Did being this close to each other affect him as powerfully as it did her? She *had* to know. *She had to!* No sooner had she recognized her need than she saw her hand lift and reach towards him.

Do you know what you're doing? her brain questioned.

'It's already broken,' he said. Then he winked, adding cheerfully, 'So look at it this way. If I stuff up, you'll never know the difference!'

Her hand froze midway between them, then fell back to her side like a lead weight, yet nothing could have been heavier than her heart. She'd unwittingly voiced the doubts in her mind aloud, but the only thing Craig had been thinking about was the air- conditioner....

In the muted light, it took a few moments of confused blinking for Taylor to realize she'd dozed off on the sofa. When she turned her head, she was only an inch away from an incredibly handsome face.

Craig's face. He was crouched beside the sofa and his voice was whisper soft as he brushed strands of sleep-strayed hair from her face. 'I thought I'd better wake you before I turned in, or you'd end up spending the entire night here.'

'What...what time is it?'

'Almost midnight.' His fingers skimmed her neck and she shivered. 'Hold still a sec,' he advised. 'You've a bit of hair twisted around your earring.'

She stilled. Not because he'd asked, but because he was so close. As his fingers closed over her ear lobe, she wondered if it wasn't the most highly sensitized part of her anatomy; awareness was sparking in every part of her body and even her scalp tingled. Though he smelt shower fresh, he hadn't shaved, and she was near enough to distinguish each and every whisker darkening his jaw. The strength she saw there seemed incongruous with the gentle touch on her ear.

'There,' he said. 'All fixed. No more tangles.'

Not in her hair perhaps, but her insides were a mass of tight, tiny knots. He slipped his fingers into her hair, watching as if fascinated by his own actions.

'Craig...'

He gave no indication he'd heard her broken whisper of his name, appearing almost trancelike as he combed his fingers to the ends of her hair, then let them trail along her cheek. She hardly dared breathe for fear she'd jerk him back to reality and he'd move from her. But it was impossible to retract the gasp she emitted as his thumb roamed over her lips.

He smiled. Then gave a soft, ironic laugh.

'You know, Tay, I've spent nearly every night here lying in my bed trying to figure out ways to get from it into yours. And then trying to imagine how to make love to you with that bloody cast on!'

He was looking at her as if expecting some response, but words failed Taylor. Her brain failed her, along with her lungs and every other vital organ in her body except her heart. And *that* was pounding so violently she was certain death was imminent.

'But you know what?'

Somehow she managed to shake her head.

'You were right.' Abandoning her face, he took her hand, exploring it with both his touch and his eyes— eyes that when they lifted back to hers were sincere. 'Satisfying though it would have been, our making love *would* have confused the past with the present. At least now when I leave tomorrow, I'll *know* my feelings are steeped in the stark realities of today not fantasy shadows of yesterday.'

Sighing as if relieved at getting everything off his chest, he kissed her forehead. It felt like the dismissal it was, his ensuing grimace-like smile a consolation prize or an encouragement award.

She watched him walk away. After three steps, he paused and turned back to give her a satisfied smirk. 'By the way, I fixed the air-conditioner. Notice how much cooler it is in here now?'

Irony wielded the knife bone deep. No blood flowed. But then ice couldn't.

Say something! her frozen heart demanded, a tremor of despair rolling through her body. Say *anything*, but don't let him see you fall apart. Dammit, Taylor! Endure the pain without tears and at least salvage your pride! *Speak*! Open your mouth and *speak*!

'I've decided to take you up on your job offer,' she heard herself say, and when he physically started, added, 'It's too late to change your mind or the terms now!'

'Why would I do that?'

She turned from the semi-puzzled smile accompanying his words as her vision began to blur; panic gripped her when a movement behind her suggested he was going to pursue the question. He didn't.

'Right. Well. I'm off to bed. Good night, Tay. I'll see you in the morning.'

Pursing her mouth against her pain, she made no response. Within seconds he was gone from the room. Within hours he'd be gone from the house.

CHAPTER FOURTEEN

As TAYLOR poured her third cup of coffee, she was pleased to note she didn't splash it over the table as she had with her previous efforts. Another twenty or so pots and her nerves would be as steady as a microsurgeon's. *If the grating sound of Craig whisking a spoon in his cup didn't drive her insane beforehand!*

'Craig,' she said, 'I think the sugar's dissolved by now.'

The stirring continued. Either he was ignoring her or totally preoccupied with his own thoughts, but his behaviour was light years away from that of the man she regarded as more mentally alert first thing in the morning than anyone breathing! Yet his distraction wasn't the only puzzling aspect to his demeanour; his eyes lacked their usual early-morning zest, his hair was damp in just-shampooed disarray and his tie hung undone like a maroon snake against the whiteness of his shirt. It was the only time Taylor had seen him arrive at breakfast on a workday not immaculately groomed for the office and it was almost time for him to drop Mel off at school.

'Have you told Melanie the plaster comes off today?' he asked suddenly.

They were the first words he'd uttered since coming downstairs, but he didn't halt the stirring and remained oblivious to her irritated glare.

'No,' she said, 'I haven't told her. I didn't want her going off to school upset. This afternoon will be soon enough.' *Too soon.*

'You're probably right....'

'But...you don't think so.'

'She's not stupid, Taylor. She'll ask where you're going the minute you get in the car with us.'

'I'm not going with you.'

There was instant silence as his hand stilled in the process of stirring the coffee. Taylor would've cheered had his chilling gaze not frozen her vocal cords.

'What do you mean you're not coming with us?' Brown eyes seemed to push her back in her chair. 'You're not going to the hospital?'

'I'm going by cab.'

'Don't be so bloody stupid! I'll drive you!'

Taylor had expected opposition, but she hadn't expected anger.

'Craig,' she said reasonably, 'you've just pointed out why that isn't a good idea. Mel will—'

'Then I'll damn well take her to school and come back for you! Your appointment isn't until eleven o'clock anyway.'

'Yes, I know, but you'll be late for work—'

'Dammit, Taylor! I *own* the bloody place. I can do what I like!' Leaping to his feet, he snatched up his coffee cup and drained it in one gulp. 'I'll take Mel, then come back for you,' he told her. 'And you damn well better be here when I do! *Understood*?'

Craig didn't wait for a response to his order and for that reason he wasn't sure if it was relief or surprise that rushed through him thirty minutes later when, having taken Mel to school, he returned as Taylor hobbled out of the downstairs bathroom.

She wore an ankle-length denim skirt and a silky navy singlet-like thing. He wasn't sure if it was the latest in street wear or underwear, but it was sexy as hell; more so because she was braless beneath it. He swallowed hard in an effort to suppress his body's stirrings.

'You're dressed?' *Like you really want to know the answer to that, Adams*! an inner voice rebuked.

'I... I won't be long,' she said. A faint tinge of rose in her cheeks, she quickly lowered her gaze, moving with awkward haste towards her room. The reaction made him feel like a jerk.

'Tay?' She glanced over her shoulder. 'I'm sorry I spat the dummy this morning. It's just...'

'Yes?'

He shook his head. 'Never mind. Like I said, take your time.'

She entered the family room a short time later, the navy silk number replaced by a faded denim shirt tied at the waist and unbuttoned just enough for the shadow between her breasts to taunt him. He forced his eyes back to the newspaper in his hand in a futile attempt to ignore the anxiety gnawing at him.

'Um, Craig...about resuming work at the office...?' Her voice was hesitant. 'I think starting Monday would be pushing it. With the leg, I mean. Would you mind if I started the following week?'

He minded like hell! It mean that after he packed his gear tonight it would be nine days before he saw her again. *Nine long, agonizing days*!

'No, that's fine. It'll give me a chance to sort out how we'll divide the work between us.'

Her agreeing nod caused a piece of hair to flop across one eye, and the movement of her breasts as she lifted her hand to push it aside tightened both his gut and his throat. He headed to the sink, at that moment almost as desperate for water as he was for her. Only the water was an option.

'I'm flexible as to what I do,' he heard her say. 'Provided it fits in with my being able to take Mel to and from school.'

'Good,' he said. 'Then perhaps we can discuss dividing the time we spend with Melanie? Because *I* may not be quite so flexible. Don't think because I haven't pushed you about it that I've changed my mind.'

The flash of pain in her green eyes made him regret his words. Dammit, Adams! he told himself. Haven't you worked out yet that by hurling darts at her you're only crucifying yourself!

'I didn't think you would.' She lifted her chin as if daring him to throw another verbal punch. 'Actually, I've come up with an ideal solution regarding that.'

'And that is?'

'Well . . .' Taylor paused and cleared her throat. She'd only made her decision last night, and voicing it aloud was difficult, but she knew putting off doing so wouldn't make it any easier. Both Craig and Melanie deserved to know where things stood. 'Melanie can sleep over every third weekend at your place. And spend one night a week with you so long as you have her home by say, ten.' Self-conscious under his frowning scrutiny, she hurried on. 'You can choose any day except Tuesday. Now I'm well again, I'll resume taking her to ballet on Tue—'

'She hates ballet,' he cut in flatly. 'She wants to take up trampolining.'

Taylor blinked. 'She does? She never told me that.'

He shrugged, then drained his glass. 'Well, that's what she told *me*. I checked around and there's trampoline instruction at the local Police Citizens Youth Club on Thursday evenings. I think if she's keen to try it, we should let her. I could take her.'

'Oh.'

What else could she say? This was the part she'd been having problems coming to terms with—letting someone else have a say in what was right for Melanie. That meant having to surrender five years of absolute control on decisions regarding her daughter's future. It hurt, too, that Melanie had expressed her wishes to Craig and not her.

'Well,' he said, 'what do you think?'

'Er . . . I think we better go. I don't want to have this cast on a second longer than necessary.'

'*About the trampolining.*'

Propped against the sink with his arms folded across his chest, he seemed to expect an immediate answer and she didn't have one.

'Can we talk about this later, Craig? I doubt you've given the matter much thought and I'm anxious to get to the hospital.'

He pushed himself upright and snatched up his keys. 'Sure, let's go! God forbid anything should delay your regaining your full mobility and independence! *Let alone listening to parental input from a rank amateur like me*!'

He was in the car and revving the engine before Taylor even reached the front door.

The drive to the hospital was completed in stony silence. Cocooned in her own thoughts, Taylor registered none of the familiar landmarks they passed *en route* and it wasn't until the wail of an ambulance siren tore at her ears that she became aware they'd arrived. When Craig stopped the car outside the out-patients' entrance contrary to a dozen signs, she quickly reached for her crutches with one hand and the seat-belt clasp with the other.

'I'll park the car, then wait for you in Reception.'

'There's no need for you to do that,' she protested. 'I could be a while. I can catch a cab home.'

'Look,' he said wearily, both hands gripping the steering wheel, 'you can't expect to be fully functional ten minutes after the cast comes off.'

Gazing into his handsome face, Taylor felt the tenuous grip she'd kept on her emotions falter. Driving here, she'd been imagining a future where Craig had a paramount role as a part-time father to Mel and as a business partner with her, but no matter how hard she tried, she couldn't feel happy with the scenario. Yet that was all she could look forward to now. Lord, she'd handled things so badly! She'd had the chance to show him they could be a loving and caring family and she'd blown it! She'd blown it because she'd allowed her own stupid pride to blind her to what was really important—the present and the future, *not the past*. She'd sanctimoniously told Craig she didn't want the past getting tangled with the present when in fact it had been unavoidable. She'd rejected love in favour of trust and in doing so shot herself in the foot!

While he was now content with a mature, platonic relationship, she craved *more*. Oh, not the volatile sensual passion of their youth! But a relationship based on a more durable stable love. A love that could handle the emotional wear and tear of marriage and parenthood rather than a fragile one that could slip from their grasp and be easily crushed underfoot. Her own maturity had taught her she now wanted a relationship that had the textured warmth and softness of crushed velvet rather than the cool smoothness of silk. But it was too late.

From today, she'd have to settle for seeing him only for a few hours each week, perhaps doing nothing more than exchanging a few brief pleasantries when he called to collect Melanie. Though she knew the little girl would be devastated when she learned Craig was moving out, the sadness she felt on her daughter's behalf paled when compared to the desolation within her own heart. Unlike her, at least Melanie would have Craig's love.

'What's the matter?'

The question intruded on her thoughts. She blinked, surprised to find Craig out of the still-idling car and holding her door open.

'Taylor, I'm stopped in a No Standing zone. If you don't get out of the car, I'm likely to wind up with a ticket.'

'Uh? Oh!' She shook her head to pull herself together. 'Sorry.'

'Are you OK?'

The concern in his voice touched her, then she remembered she was only minutes away from having both the cast and him removed from her daily life.

'I'm fine.' She glossed over the lie with what she hoped was a convincing smile. 'Look, if waiting for me isn't going to inconvenience you, I'd be glad of a lift home.'

One hour later, she left the doctor and made her way back to reception with her heart pounding in her throat. Taking a steadying breath, she scanned the waiting room until she sighted Craig.

He was sitting in a molded-plastic chair, his legs stretched out and his ankles crossed. The knot in his tie was a slack two inches below his unbuttoned collar and a stray lock of hair fell across his forehead. He appeared engrossed in a back issue of *Popular Mechanics*.

Pushing against the wave of apprehension that threatened to paralyse her, Taylor moved towards him. 'Like I said, there's still a lot of grease in your blood.'

His head came up at the sound of her voice, then in one motion the magazine was tossed aside and he was on his feet.

'What the hell! You've still got the cast on!'

'For another week at least.'

He frowned, studying her through narrowed eyes, his jaw rigid. 'There's no problem, is there? I mean, they said it'd be four weeks.'

'Four or *five* weeks. There's no problem except it looks like being five weeks instead of four.'

'You must be disappointed.'

'I'll just have to put up with it, I guess.'

Apart from his initial look of dismay when he'd seen the cast, Craig's demeanour showed nothing of his feelings at this unexpected turn of events. But Taylor was compelled to offer him an escape.

'Don't feel you have to stay because of this,' she said. 'You've already put yourself out enough. You can still move out tonight. I'll understand.'

His face tightened. 'I promised Mel I'd stay until the cast was off. I won't be leaving till then.' Shoving his

hand into his pocket, he pulled out his keys. 'Stay here.
I'll bring the car round.'

As he helped Taylor into the car, Craig announced he'd
decided not to go to the office and suggested they have
lunch together. Surprise made her slow to reply, but Craig
apparently interpreted her silence as reluctance.

'It's pretty pointless to do anything else, really,' he
said, sliding behind the steering wheel. 'By the time I
drop you home and get back to the office, I'm not going
to get much work done before I have to pick Mel up.
Besides, neither of us has had lunch and you can
probably use some cheering up.' When she still didn't
reply, he risked a glance away from the traffic. 'You
didn't have other plans, did you?'

She shook her head. 'Not any more. I was hoping to
take a long walk on the beach, but that's out of the
question with this.' She tapped the cast. 'Still on.'

'That's what you wanted to do? Go to the beach?'

'Yeah, I've always equated the beach with freedom.'
She smiled. 'After the restrictions of the last month, a
trip to the beach seemed symbolic.'

At her word, he executed a sudden right-hand turn
that had her gripping the dashboard. '*Craig*! What are
you doing?'

'You want the beach. You've got it!'

'But I can't go tramping through sand with a cast on!'

'True. But I know this great little restaurant on the
beach at Balmoral. The view is fantastic, the seafood
second to none.' He flashed her a smile. 'Trust me. It'll
cheer you up!'

Though his smile warmed her all the way to her toes,
Taylor was feeling anything but cheerful. *Trust* wasn't
the word she wanted to hear right now.

The view was everything he promised. Situated right
on the beach, the restaurant made the most of its lo-
cation by letting French doors substitute for windows

on the ocean side of the building and allowing patrons seated inside the same visual spectacle as those who favoured alfresco dining. Taylor knew the food would be every bit as delicious as it looked, but she also knew it would take a miracle to keep it in her furiously churning stomach and she was hardly in a position to ask God for miracles. Her vision blurred, but she didn't for a minute believe the cause was the bright March sun reflecting off the water.

'Not hungry?'

The question jerked her gaze from the ocean view and back to the man opposite. She blinked to clear her vision and was instantly aware of the tension lines bracketing his mouth and the disapproving angle of his eyebrows.

'Ye—' She stopped mid-lie. 'Not really. I'm sorry.'

'Sorry you're not hungry or sorry you're stuck with me as a house guest for another week?'

'No!' Her denial was loud and attracted the attention of nearby diners. Blushing, she lowered both her head and her voice. 'It's not that. And you're hardly a house guest. You've cooked all the meals, shopped, played chauffeur to Mel and me.' She offered a weak smile. 'I want you to know I'm very grateful. I really appreciate—'

'Gee, Taylor, just what every guy wants to hear! That he's helpful around the house! Keep throwing that sort of flattery about and I'll get a big head!'

His sarcasm was too much for her to handle. 'Oh, grow), Craig! I've had a rotten day. I don't need your laying a guilt trip on me because I didn't eat everything on my plate!'

He leaned over the table. 'You haven't eaten *anything*! All you've done is sit there staring at the ocean and holding your knife and fork! OK, so the plaster has to stay on another week. Big deal! It's not the end of the world! I thought this would cheer you up!'

'Well, it hasn't! Why bring me here, Craig? Why *here* of all places? This is where we celebrated lunch after Adams Relief signed its first national company as a client! Did you think I'd forget something like that? You throw our past in my face and expect me to feel *cheered*?' Past trying to keep her emotions in check, she put both arms on the table and leaned towards him. 'News flash, Craig! You *haven't* cheered me up! All you've done is churn up a lot of old memories that right now hurt like hell!'

He trapped her wrist in his hand. 'Listen, don't think you've cornered the market on hurt, lady! But unlike you, I'm at least honest enough to accept we shared some good times in the past. The day we came here was one of them. I thought maybe, *just maybe*, the last month would have gone some way towards laying the foundation of at least a *friendship* between us! But you don't even want that, do you?'

Biting her lip to keep her sobs silent, Taylor studied her plate. Suddenly Craig uttered an indistinct curse and rose angrily to his feet.

'Let's get out of here! Before I make an even bigger ass of myself.' He snatched her crutches from beneath the table, but shook his head when she reached for them. 'Hang on to me,' he said.

Head bent, she waited as the bill was settled, then allowed herself to be guided through the maze of tables to the door. Craig's grip on her arm was the only thing keeping her balanced. The moment they stepped out into the sunlit car park, he turned her into his chest and wrapped his arms around her.

'I'm sorry. I—'

His words opened the floodgates of Taylor's overwrought emotions. Nuzzling into his chest, she surrendered to the need to cry.

'Aw, honey!' She heard the crutches drop to the concrete seconds before strong male arms tightened around her.

She had no idea how long she stood sobbing within the security of Craig's arms, but even when she was too spent to manage more than a hiccuped, half-strangled gasp, she pressed closer; the thought of breaking contact with the warm strength of his body and the touch of his hand on the back of her head was too awful to contemplate. But it seemed bitterly ironic that, besieged by pain and confusion, she sought comfort from the man at the source of her grief. It occurred to her she was deceiving him yet again, but even that wasn't enough to make her step away. That her need for him could entice her to be less than honest was a weakness she'd have to rise above in the future, but not yet. Not for a little while.

'Feeling better?' he asked.

The warmth of his palm stroking over her back made it easy to at least answer that question truthfully; in his arms everything was better. She nodded. 'I...I'm sor—'

He gave her a gentle squeeze. 'Ssshh. I'm the one who should be apologizing. Bringing you here when you were already upset was dumb.'

Pushing away from his chest, she looked up, shaking her head. She even managed a watery smile. 'No, it wasn't. It was thoughtful.'

He gave her a sceptical look. 'It reduced you to tears and me to an aggressive horse's rear. Heaven forbid I should ever get *thoughtless*.' Her tiny chuckle brought his hands to her face. 'Taylor, I'm not asking you to forget the bad stuff I put you through. Or even to forgive me for it. All I want is that you not block out the good stuff. That's what my parents did and I can tell you I don't want Melanie to grow up with the bitterness and hate that I did.' His eyes bored into hers. 'You *must* remember the good times, Tay,' he urged. 'The laughter, the loving, how—'

'I remember.' She touched his cheek. 'But sometimes they hurt more than the bad, Craig. Everything's different—'

'I know. But even though it's easier to start from now, we have to accept that we *had* a past. We can't paper over it.' He kissed her palm. 'I want us to be friends, Tay. But *old* friends, not new ones.'

What he asked for was so much less than what she wanted, yet much more than she deserved. And God knew she wasn't strong enough to walk away from what few scraps he offered.

She nodded. 'Me, too. I want us to be friends, too.'

But living with her lies would be harder than telling them.

CHAPTER FIFTEEN

CRAIG'S hope that in the wake of their frank, emotive conversation Taylor would be more relaxed around him, when Melanie wasn't there to act as a buffer between them, was short-lived. Even over dinner, when Mel *had* been present, Taylor was silent and withdrawn. It may not have been apparent to a stranger, but Craig was too attuned to subtle whispers of her body language not to notice; she'd barely eaten a bite, she didn't offer responses with the perfect timing of someone who was aware of what was going on around them and her laughter had a forced, brittle ring to it.

After tucking Melanie into bed, she'd joined him in front of the television, but though she looked at the screen, he knew she wasn't absorbing what was happening; during a commercial break, he'd flicked channels from the British drama they'd been viewing to a Western, and she hadn't even commented. He was through suffering in silent ignorance!

'OK, Tay,' he said, switching the TV off with the remote control. 'What's up?'

'Uh?'

'I said, *what's up*?'

'Er, nothing. Nothing's up. Why would anything be up?' At least she had the good grace to look away as she lied.

'Tay, I'm not *completely* stupid. You've been distracted and edgy all evening. You turn away when I look at you. Hell, if I've done something to upset you, for God's sake tell me what it is so I'll at least *know* why I'm getting the cold shoulder!'

She swung her head towards him. 'You haven't done anything!' At his disbelieving stare, she again averted her gaze. 'I'm not upset with you. I... I'm not. Really.'

He heard the slight quiver in her voice and cursed. But, realizing his anger wouldn't help matters, he forced himself to remain calm.

'All right, if it's not me, what is it? You're upset about *something*.'

She opened her mouth, but shut it again without speaking. Dammit! Why couldn't she trust him enough to tell him what was troubling her? What did she think he would do? Oh, he knew what he *wanted* to do—kiss her until she came to her senses! But unfortunately that wasn't an option. He sighed and tilted her face to his.

'Tay, *tell* me. Maybe I can help you.'

Her head shook ever so slightly, her eyelids lowering until her lashes made dark arcs on her skin. Her flawless beauty had always fascinated him. It still did. Her soft, shapely lips became the main focus of his attention as desire built swift and hard within him. He'd already held her in his arms once today and fought the urge to kiss her; he seriously doubted he could do it again.

'Talking things out might help you put things in perspective,' he said, thinking it was also the only thing that might stop him from ravishing her.

'I... I can't.'

As her mouth formed the words, the movement of her tongue echoed deep inside himself. He summoned every ounce of intestinal strength he possessed to hold himself away from her. If friendship was all she wanted, he'd be the best damned friend ever created—even if it killed him! And he was beginning to think there was every chance it would.

'We're friends, right?' he heard himself say as his senses swam in the scent of her. 'Friends share their problems. They *trust* each other...'

She flinched, then squeezed her eyes shut. 'I know. But this is something I can't talk about. Not... not to you.'

Furious his self-control had been for nothing, he jumped to his feet and gave his frustration free rein. 'Fine! Wallow in your own misery, Taylor, if that's what you want! But I'm outta here! Forget our being *friends*! Friendship with you is too bloody hard to take!'

'*What*?' She looked shell-shocked. 'Where are you going?'

'Out! For a walk with man's best friend! Bernie's behaviour might be wayward, but at least it's consistent! And being with him doesn't burn at my guts!'

'Well, well! And just who is walking who here?'

After being dragged eight blocks in the dark by an unruly St Bernard, seeing Liz O'Shea getting out of her car as he re-entered the front yard was the last thing Craig needed tonight.

'Still,' the redhead went on, 'you executive types need exercise. You're prime candidates for stress and diet-related heart attacks.'

'Do me a favour, Liz,' Craig said. 'Hold your breath while you're waiting for me to have mine.'

The woman's throaty chuckle followed him as he led Bernie around to the side entrance of the house and turned him loose in the backyard. Surprisingly, she stood waiting while he locked the gate.

'It's a pity I didn't know you were coming, Liz,' he remarked. 'If I had, I could have coordinated walking the dog with your visit and spared you the anguish of my presence while you saw Taylor.'

A wide smile greeted his words. 'Assuming, of course, I'm here to see *Taylor*. Who's to say I'm not here to see you?'

'Yeah, right. And you don't hate my guts, either.'

'I don't hate your guts, Craig. I never did. I simply didn't believe you ever loved Taylor as much as she loved you. Perhaps if you'd followed her to South Australia, you might have convinced me otherwise.'

There was a note of challenge in Liz O'Shea's voice; there always was when she spoke to him. But, knowing this discussion was long overdue, Craig resisted the temptation of going inside and avoiding it. Instead, he propped himself against the bonnet of Liz's Volvo, showing his intention to finally have it out. After a few moments, Liz assumed a similar position. It was then Craig spoke.

'I didn't go after Taylor because *she left me*. It wasn't my love for her that was in question. It was hers for me. She put her feelings in writing and I got the message loud and clear. I sure didn't need the agony of hearing it a second time.'

'I doubt you would have. The fact is she never stopped loving you.' Liz gave Craig no time to question her comment. 'Taylor went through a very traumatic time, Craig. She didn't know what she wanted or what she needed. I think secretly she hoped you *would* go after her, but emotionally, she needed the breathing space.'

'Right,' he said drily. 'So why didn't she come back when she got her emotional second wind?'

'She has.'

It took a second for Liz's words to sink in, but Craig couldn't allow himself to believe them. 'She came back because Melanie needed a father.'

'Women with Taylor's looks and money can find fathers for their kids without crossing half a continent to do it.'

Even to his own ears, there was something strained in the ironic laugh he gave. 'Liz, much as I wish otherwise, there's nothing you can say that will convince me Taylor loves me.'

'Not even if I tell you I'm here to take her plaster off?'

'*Take her plaster off*? What the hell are you rabbiting on about, Liz? The cast has to stay on for another...' His voice trailed off in the face of Liz's amused shaking head.

'There was no reason the cast couldn't have come off today. If Taylor had been worried about the sudden lack of support, the hospital would have given her a knee brace that attaches with Velcro. The fact is, she *begged* Dr Kalvaris to leave the plaster on.'

What Liz was saying made no sense. 'But...*why*? It's driving her crazy! She can't stand—'

'What she can't stand,' Liz cut in, opening the passenger door of her car and reaching inside, 'is the thought of you moving out. Keeping the cast on kept that at bay a little longer.'

Assaulted by a swarm of emotions, Craig was unable to suck sufficient air into his lungs to speak. Standing, he turned and pressed his palms against the metal of the car, extending his arms until the muscles in them strained from the effort, then drew a series of deep, slow breaths. *Taylor wanted him to stay? It couldn't be true.*

'Are you sure about this, Liz? I mean, did she *tell* you?'

His heart stopped when the redhead shook her head.

'That she loves you? No. That she begged them to leave the cast on? Yes. She phoned me a little while ago howling her heart out because she could live with the cast, but *not* the guilt of deception. Or some equally hysterical romantic phrase! So,' she said, jiggling her medical bag, 'I'm here in my medical capacity. But you, Craig...'

She gave him such a kind smile, Craig wondered who she'd borrowed it from.

'...are the only one who can rid her of the guilt. Now, unfortunately, I've got to go in there and tell her I've been called back to the hospital, so that cast'll have to stay on till at least tomorrow.'

'Let me do both!' At Liz's incredulous expression, Craig elaborated, 'Let me cure her guilt *and* take off the cast!'

'What? Let *you* take the cast off?' She looked aghast.

'Yeah. Why not? If we were in the middle of nowhere, I'd have to do it.'

'But you've never used a plaster saw in your life!'

'Yeah, but I've seen them used and I know how they work. They're a little rectangular thing with a vibrating blade that kind of chews through the plaster. It's a bit like a power grinder.' Liz's expression was one of disbelief, but Craig wasn't put off by it. 'Liz, I can do this! I'm used to handling power tools. I was a mechanic before—'

'Sure, and Christian Barnard knows his way around hearts, but I wouldn't trust him to adjust my carburettor!'

'But don't you see?' Craig pressed her. 'That's why it's important *I* do this. That's what it's all about.'

'*Carburettors*?'

'No, Liz! *Trust.*' For a presumably intelligent woman, she was incredibly dense! 'It's about trusting our love. In the past, Taylor and I didn't trust our love enough. We both thought there was a limit on what we could give and get back!'

He grasped her shoulders. '*Please, Liz, let me do this*! I swear if I can't handle it, or if Tay doesn't want me to do it, I'll call you. Please?'

'Craig, it makes more sense if I simply walk in there, whip off the cast and go.'

'But it won't prove anything!' He racked his brain for the words to make Liz understand. He *knew* in his gut this was the right thing to do, yet how did you translate gut feelings into words a person who'd been suspicious of you for years could believe?

'Look, Liz, neither Taylor nor I will be risking anything if *you* do it—'

'But there's usually nothing *risky* about taking a cast off.'

'Exactly! Which is why I *can* do it! The thing is, while there's no *physical* risk, emotionally we'd both be showing how much trust we have in our love—me by wanting to do it and Taylor by letting me. It would be like a declaration of faith in each other.'

'More like a declaration of lunacy!'

'Please, Liz, I know we've never seen eye to eye in the past. But you have to know that I'd never do anything to hurt Taylor. *Never again.*'

Stepping back, Liz sighed and shook her head. 'I'm not sure which of the two of us is more stupid,' she said. 'You for suggesting this or me for going along with it. But Taylor will top us both in stupidity if she agrees! And if anything goes wrong, my career's on the line.'

Craig embraced the resigned redhead with grateful enthusiasm and even kissed her on the mouth. 'If what you've told me is true, she'll agree! And I promise, if anything, God forbid, does go wrong, no one will ever know you were involved. I'll claim I stole the plaster saw from the hospital!'

He went to kiss her again, but Liz pushed him away. 'Hey! Back off, Adams. I'm not impressed by macho displays of affection.'

'Which,' he added wryly, as she opened her medical bag, 'I suspect is one of the reasons we've always been so wary of each other.'

'Probably,' she conceded. 'You're too typically male for my liking, but for some reason, liberated though she is, Taylor always had a weakness for your brand of heavy-duty machismo.' Extracting a small box from her bag, she lifted its lid, then glanced back at Craig. 'I love Taylor. She's my best friend. Hurt her again and I'll kill you.'

'I love her, too, but too much for friendship ever to work between us. So,' he said after they'd exchanged silent, understanding smiles, 'you want to run through how this thing works?'

Whilst questioning her own sanity, Liz O'Shea explained how the plaster saw should be operated.

'Sounds simple enough,' Craig said when she'd finished.

'It has to be—so male members of the medical profession can operate it! But I've still got doubts about mechanics!'

Laughing, he held the car door open for Liz. She climbed in and wound down her window to issue final instructions.

'Look, the blade only vibrates so it's impossible to cut the skin. When the cast comes off, though, there'll probably be some wasting of the quadricep muscles at the front of the thigh and the flesh will be dry and flaky. It'll be dirty, too, because of the heat and sweating. Soap, water and moisturizer in that order should solve the problem.'

'What about sex?'

'No, that's not standard hospital procedure.'

'Very funny! I mean, is she up to it?'

She widened her eyes. 'Cute play on words, Craig. And I doubt either of you would listen if I said no, but keep things as passive as possible. She'll probably be a bit stiff.'

'She won't be the only one!' he said, laughing as Liz groaned and started the engine. 'Hey, Liz!' he called when the vehicle started to reverse. 'Thanks.'

'You just make sure you call the hospital if there are any problems at all with the cast or if Taylor complains of pain or discomfort in her leg.'

Taylor was standing at the door of her bedroom when Craig let himself in the front door. She wore an ankle-length towelling robe and a puzzled expression.

'I thought I heard Liz's car out front.'

'You did. She's just left.'

'Left! But she was going to take—' She stopped dead and swallowed; a red tinge coloured her face and neck. It was all Craig could do not to haul her into his arms.

'I know why she was here, Tay.'

'You . . . you do?'

He nodded, taking the necessary steps to bring him directly in front of her. 'You asked her to come over and take the cast off.'

Under his gaze, Taylor felt both the hot tingle of arousal and a chill sense of paralysis. She wasn't sure if it was because he was emitting mixed messages or because she was a hair's breadth from a nervous breakdown.

'Why, Taylor?'

'Wh-why what?'

Reaching out, he slid one side of her hair behind her ear. She gripped the door jamb with white-knuckled ferocity as his fingers skimmed her skin.

'Why pretend the cast had to stay on and then change your mind?'

'Because I couldn't keep up the deceit.'

A wry smile slipped across his previously unreadable face. 'That answers the changed-your-mind part of the question, but not the first.'

Feeling as if she was about to throw herself off a cliff, Taylor heaved a huge breath and shut her eyes. 'Because I love you. Because I didn't want you to lea—'

Strong male arms closed around her, cutting off both her words and air and lifting her from the ground!

'You idiot! Don't you know you only had to ask me?'

Not trusting her hearing, Taylor lifted her lashes. The brightness of his grin nearly blinded her, but the love burning in his brown eyes was intense enough to penetrate all her senses. She felt it all the way to her soul.

'I *love* you, Tay. I love you more than life itself!'

Tears washed down her face as he lowered her to the floor without loosening his hold and she tasted them as his mouth unerringly found hers. She clung to him as the kiss transposed itself from tender to aggressive and the million emotions in between. It was broken by sighs of relief, moans of desire and joyful snickers of laughter and it went on...and on.

Taylor arched back, tilting her head to accommodate Craig's hot, hungry mouth when it abandoned her lips to venture down over her chin and along her throat, and groaned as the movement brought her firmly against the hardness of his arousal. Unsteadied, she grasped at the waist of his jeans, holding tight as if dangling from a twelfth-storey ledge where to let go was to perish. And then she felt the stability of a wall against her back and somehow her robe was untied and shoved from her shoulders to drop at her feet.

Craig rested his forehead against hers, and they stared at each other, matching each other ragged breath for ragged breath, while her fingers released the buttons of his shirt. When he cupped her nipple-erect breasts through her oversize T-shirt, she trembled with the force of her desire, but it was he who groaned.

'Oh, Tay,' he muttered, scattering butterfly kisses over her face, 'I want you so badly I'm dying from it. But we've gotta slow down here, or I'll be too damn shaky to cut that cast off.'

Emerald eyes, liquid with passion, rose questioningly to his face. 'What?'

'Liz left me this thing to get it off with.' He held his breath and mentally crossed his fingers. 'That is, if you trust me to do it.'

She was frowning at him as if he'd sprouted an extra head.

'I know it sounds risky, but it's not. If Liz had any doubt about it being safe she'd never have left the thing with me. There's no way I can hurt you. It just sort of vibrates.' He searched her face for some indication he'd reassured her, but saw none.

'It *vibrates*?'

He nodded.

'And *Liz* gave it to you?'

'Yeah.'

'To...*get it off with*?'

He nodded.

'And this thing is called...?'

'A plaster saw.'

'Oh, I see!' She gave him a dazzling smile. 'A *plaster saw*! Of course I trust you to use a *plaster saw* on me.'

Craig sighed and kissed her thoroughly, then stepped back, intending to retrieve the saw from outside the front door. 'Thank heaven for that. You have no idea how relieved I am.'

'*You're* relieved!' She laughed, eyes sparkling. 'For a minute there, I thought I was being offered a mechanical substitute for you.'

His brain was a tad slow comprehending her words, but understanding brought a mixture of disbelief and male possessiveness. 'You thought *what*? *No way*!'

'My sentiments exactly,' she whispered, her hand snaking out to grab the waistband of his jeans and tug him back against her. 'This is all I want.'

Craig's legs nearly buckled under him when her fingers closed around him; the intimacy of her touch sending an electric charge through his body. As she pampered him with slow, steady strokes, a moan of pleasure burst from his throat and he was unable to stop himself from seizing her mouth. Eventually, giddy with desire and on the verge of exploding, he dragged himself away from the taste of her.

'Tay, honey,' he rasped, 'if we don't stop now, I'm going to melt in your hand.'

'So?' she asked, looking innocently wide-eyed despite the fact her hand was wantonly disregarding his caution.

'The last thing I want is for either of us to die of frustration before you cut this plaster off me.'

He grinned. 'Ah! So you want me for my body, uh?'

'No...' Her face became serious, her eyes looking into his with an intensity that made his breath catch. 'I want you for the rest of my life.'

CHAPTER SIXTEEN

HAD anyone told Taylor having a cast cut from her leg could be a sensual experience, she'd have called them insane. But not after tonight.

Though they'd brought each other to rapid physical release in the doorway of her bedroom, she and Craig were both aware a far more gratifying experience still awaited them. Anticipation of the ultimate union of their love and need for one another built with every passing minute and each exchange of glances as she sat on the floor, draped only in her robe, while Craig manoeuvred the plaster saw over her encased leg.

Her heart had swelled with love when he painstakingly stopped cutting every inch or so to ask if she was OK; if she was *certain* she didn't want him to call Liz to come over and finish it. She'd assured him she didn't, that she had absolute confidence in him, and while it was obvious her response pleased him, his frustration with the task, which was taking much longer than Liz had predicted, was highlighted by muttered curses and comments. '*Maybe this wasn't such a hot idea. At this rate, it's probably gonna take all night!*' She found his impatience to get the job over was as sweet as it was arousing, but not as arousing as when he carried her to the bathroom to bathe her leg.

The first sight of her grubby limb with its muscle-slack thigh had caused her to gasp and feminine vanity made her quickly cover it within the lengths of her robe. Yet he washed away her self-consciousness with nothing more than a cake of soap, a shower of warm water and a pair of the hottest hands she could have imagined!

175

When he stripped naked and handed the wash cloth to her, she was shaking so much she could barely hold it, much less stand up. Yet her trembling attempts to lather him in suds soon became a wanton exploration of the hard planes and muscles of his body. Beneath her palms, the sleek, soapy smoothness of his skin was intoxicating, and she suspected the steam clouding the glass of the shower recess came not from the heat of the water but from the heat of her body as his head-to-toe kisses sizzled her blood.

Desperate for the release only he could grant, she instinctively tried to wrap her legs around him, but a furious protest from the rusty muscles in her right leg aborted the action. She swore and strong male hands clasped her protectively closer.

Taylor tried to assure him her epithet had sprung more from frustration than genuine pain. But he wasn't convinced, immediately turning off the shower and towelling her dry before carrying her to her bed. However, the sight of his naked perfection standing over her with a bottle of moisturizer in his hands was making her damp in places a towel didn't belong.

'What's that for?' she asked.

He sat down on the edge of the mattress, his eyes running appreciatively over her nakedness. 'Your leg,' he said, pausing to again visually massage her body. 'To start with...'

With a slightly shaking hand, he trickled a stream of milky white liquid from her thigh to her ankle. The coolness of it against her skin might have made her catch her breath, but she suspected the feel of Craig's mouth against her breast was the more likely cause; the action incited her back to arch up from the bed even while he massaged her thigh with a firm, downward pressure.

His lips travelled from her nipple to the underside of her breast, then descended over her ribs to her belly, the downward direction of his mouth in perfect proportion to the progress of the moisturizer and his hand down her leg. Her mind calculated where his mouth would be when his fingers wrapped themselves around her ankle, causing white-hot heat to scorch through her. Gripping his shoulders, she closed her eyes to prepare for the rush of pleasure she knew was coming, yet it wasn't enough. *Nothing* could have readied her for the unimaginable tenderness of his lips or the calligraphic delicacy of his tongue. She clutched at his hair to draw his head up.

'No—no solo trips to heaven,' she said when he stopped and gave her a look of puzzled disappointment. 'We go together...and we go as one.'

Craig's body nearly disintegrated at her softly spoken words. Drawing a deep breath to stabilize himself, he moved to lie beside her.

'That could be awkward with your leg stiff,' he warned, pushing her hair from her face. 'Liz advised passive.'

She grinned. 'Yeah, but Liz doesn't know what she's talking about.'

To Craig, she had never tasted so innocently sweet or so brazenly wild as she lured his lips and tongue into an erotic waltz that nearly snapped the thin thread of his control. The feel of her hands roaming over him gave both pleasure and pain; one minute her fingernails were trailing lightly along his spine, the next her hands were roughly kneading his shoulder and upper arm.

Reality, like time, became irrelevant as their passion both reactivated old familiar sensations and led to the discovery of new ones. Wallowing in the luxury of having every centimetre of Taylor's flesh freely available to his hungry mouth and hands, Craig explored her with detailed intimacy until they were both slick with sweat and panting. When her luminous emerald eyes opened to meet his, the breathless quality of her voice was as seductive as her words.

'Make love to me. Oh, Craig...I need you so badly....'

The break in her voice was his undoing. He could deny this woman nothing. She was his life, his heart, his very soul! Groaning his surrender, he reclaimed her mouth.

Taylor didn't know what physical action had transpired to bring them to the position where they lay on their sides facing each other, but they were so close she could feel Craig's heart beating in his chest. Her stiff leg was beneath her, but she wasn't conscious of feeling any pain. Indeed, she'd long since passed the point of being capable of any type of coherent thought, absorbed solely with the sight, scent and feel of the man holding her in his arms and the throbbing heat of him burning against her.

'I want you so bad, babe, I'm even more afraid of hurting you than I was the night I took your virginity.'

His admission was delivered in a raspy, but gentle voice. With one hand he was stroking her side up and down from armpit to knee, while his other arm was curved beneath and around her in support. But it wasn't support or gentleness Taylor's alert body craved, as his insidiously erotic fingers stoked her desire higher and higher, the course roughness of his chest teasing her erect, burning nipples. She'd been denied this man's loving for nearly six years and the result was a hot, fevered ache, which could no longer be appeased with the tender ministrations of his lips and fingers, no matter how skilful!

With one arm effectively trapped between them, she lifted the other so she could trace his lips. 'You didn't *take* anything,' she told him, one finger probing the moist recess of his mouth. 'I *gave* you my virginity because it was *meant* for you.' Withdrawing her finger, she slid it up to his ear. 'You didn't hurt me then and you won't hurt me now.' Muttering an explicit description of what he wanted to do to her, Craig attempted to claim her mouth, but she pulled her head back and swung her good leg over his hip. 'So do it,' she challenged, nudging her wetness against his arousal. '*Now*!'

The command had barely burst from her tongue when the smooth, hard length of him filled her. Two gasps of pleasure united as one in the room's dim silence.

Taylor was instantly consumed by such an utter sense of rightness and completion that tears welled in her eyes. When they slipped down her face, Craig caught them on his tongue, his nearness revealing the glitter of liquid in his own dark eyes and prompting her to lay an unsteady palm over his cheek.

Yet apart from that they didn't move or speak, for there were no words to describe the impact or the import of this moment. Still with their gazes locked, they exchanged a spiritual vow of love so intense it caused them to shudder as one.

Awash with joy, Taylor lowered her lips to those of her one and only lover. 'Welcome home, my darling,' she whispered.

He woke hard with wanting her as he'd done a million times before, but unlike those other times the sight of her arm lying across his chest made the pain physical rather than emotionally gut-wrenching. Rolling over, he studied her face in the day's embryonic sunlight. Unable to help himself, he stroked light fingers over the smoothness of her cheek and smiled with the knowledge he would wake to her warmth and beauty every morning for the rest of his life.

He grinned, eyeing the ice tray lying by the bed; she'd ordered him into the kitchen for that at about two in the morning. Not that he'd complained. They'd made gentle, exquisite love many times during the night, and incredibly, each time had seemed better than the last. They'd also talked, *really* talked, about their fears and doubts of the past and their beliefs and hopes for the future. And they'd talked of their love; how in the past they'd assumed it to have limitations, when in fact they now recognized it was boundless.

And, of course, they'd talked about Melanie and how they would tell her that she'd be getting a *real* father on a *permanent* basis.

Again Craig cursed the selfish stupidity that had robbed him of the first five years of his child's life. Once, he'd never imagined it possible to love anyone but Taylor; now he was unable to imagine what it had felt like *not* to love Melanie. Not only did he love Mel, but his love for her was as strong and undiluted as that which he felt for her mother. He still marvelled at the discovery he was not only capable of loving two people with such soul-deep intensity, but that his love for them could be so uniquely different.

'You look very thoughtful.'

He smiled at Taylor's sleep-husky interruption. 'Do I? I was pondering the intricacies of love.'

She raised an eyebrow. 'Physical or spiritual?' she enquired, walking her fingers suggestively down his chest.

'Spiritual.' He grinned at her playful pout. 'How's the leg?'

'What leg?' she responded as his hand explored the limb in question from knee to thigh. Under his skilful, teasing fingers, her desire once again began rapidly rising, but she doubted it could ever reach the heights her happiness had during the past seven hours. *Craig loved her*! Loved her as she loved him—*totally and unconditionally*!

Angling herself so she lay partially over him, she kissed a trail across his bristled jaw, then backtracked the path with her tongue. She was only halfway through the sensual exercise when he uttered a desperate moan and snared her mouth with his.

Though the pace and rhythm of his tongue was hectic, the hands grazing the curve of her back and buttocks were teasingly slow. Arousingly slow. *Insanely* slow. Finally, nearly crazy for the feel of him, she reached back and, grabbing his wrist, repositioned his hand to the juncture of her thighs.

His fingers encountered her eager wetness and Craig knew he could have this woman a million times a day and still want more. No other woman had ever aroused him so easily, quickly or deeply, because none ever could. What made Taylor special was that she engaged not simply his body, but his heart and not only when they made love, but through every minute of his life be he awake or asleep.

Examining her face for any sign of discomfort from her leg, he lifted her over him.

'Watch,' she urged softly, lowering her head as she commenced to ride him with a slow, easy rhythm.

Following her gaze, he was awestruck by the powerful emotions erupting in his heart at the sight of their intimate union. 'Being joined with you is the most incredibly beautiful...wonderful thing I...I've ever known.'

'It is for me, too,' she whispered, her head lifting as he urged her chin up with an unsteady hand. His brown eyes were liquid with love and desire as they studied her.

'I don't just mean physically, Tay,' he said. 'I mean *spiritually*. What I feel for you goes soul deep.' Grasping her hands, he kissed the inside of each wrist. 'I love you, Tay, heart and soul for all eternity.'

Taylor let her kiss tell him she already knew that....

EPILOGUE

AT THE sound of someone entering the den, Craig slid the evidence of what he was doing into the top drawer of his desk and schooled his face to innocence.

'Relax, Dad,' Melanie said, pointedly locking the door behind her. 'Mum is well and truly occupied as requested.' With a grin, his nineteen-year-old daughter perched herself on the edge of his desk. 'So show me. What did you buy her?'

Winking, he pulled the hastily concealed wrapping paper and a long black velvet box from the drawer.

'Jewellery *again*, Dad?' Melanie shook her head. 'Not terribly original for a twenty-fifth wedding anniversary.'

'This is,' he said smugly, lifting the lid of the box.

'A charm bracelet...oh, Dad, it's beautiful! I love it!'

Craig grinned. Melanie might have his colouring, but her good taste and sense of style were inherited from her mother. Not to mention her deep sentimentality. If Mel loved it even without knowing the story behind each of the solid silver charms he'd had specially made, then his choice had been a good one.

'I can't believe how delicate and intricately detailed most of the charms are....'

'All except the five weeping hearts,' he said, hearing the unspoken question in her voice. 'They represent the five years we were apart.'

Meeting his gaze with teary eyes, his daughter nodded. 'I know.'

The emotion his explanation generated in his daughter hit Craig like a punch to the gut. Skirting the desk, he took her in his arms.

'Oh, sweetheart, if I could make it up to you, I would! You'll never know how sorry I am that I wasn't there for you when I should have been—'

'Dad, I'm not upset because you weren't around when I was little.'

'I know you say that, but—'

'Daddy, it's not just something I *say* to make you feel better. *It's true*. I've long forgotten what it was like living in South Australia except that Grandpa had some kind of big black limo.' She grinned at him. 'Just the fact that I can't even recall what make it was should tell you how dim my memory is.'

Craig smiled as he was intended to, but not even the past fourteen years had completely rid him of guilt over having let both Taylor and Melanie down long ago. If giving and receiving love in abundance had been an antidote for remorse, then by rights he should have been free of the past's shadows. Unfortunately it wasn't.

'Daddy,' she persisted, touching what she'd always called his bravery badge, 'I don't even *know* anyone who can remember anything that happened before they were five or so. But I know heaps of people who at one stage or other had to sit back and watch their parents tear each other apart, cheat on one another or get divorced. I've always thought I was really lucky that you and Mum, well . . . got all that crap out of the way before it could affect me.' She kissed his cheek. 'If you want to know the truth, the earliest clear memory I have is conning you into taking me to McDonald's.'

He blinked away tears even as his chest vibrated with laughter. 'I remember. You told me how Renee's father took her there every week.'

A smug smirk best described her expression. 'Dad,' she said, taking a step backwards, 'Renee's folks were vegetarian health-food nuts. I doubt they even knew what a hamburger looked like!'

'Why you—'

'Craig! Craig, where are you?'

'Quick, it's your mother! Unlock the door while I hide her present.'

As Taylor entered, father and daughter turned from the window as if they'd been watching the hustle and bustle as a dozen workmen erected tables around the pool area of their home.

'See, Mum, I told you'd I'd find him eventually.'

The comment came from their younger daughter, fourteen-year-old Summer, and Craig fought down a smile as from behind her mother the teenager sent him a wink. Like her older sister, Summer was the image of him, and, though he'd gone through hell fearing her unplanned conception would cause Taylor the same difficulties Melanie had, her birth, thankfully, had been relatively easy by comparison. But once again, Taylor had been hospitalized early and the doctors had warned against risking a third pregnancy. Despite Taylor's efforts to get him to admit otherwise, he'd finally convinced her he had no secret desire to have a son. Nor did he. With three perfect women in his life, he knew he was luckier than he deserved to be.

'You wanted me for something, honey?' he asked, the innocence of his words belying the thoughts that merely looking at his wife generated. She was gorgeous! At forty-three, though not looking a day over thirty-five, she was more beautiful and exciting to him than she'd been at eighteen.

'Only to tell you that you'd best start dressing for the party.'

'No sweat, there's heaps of time—'

Catching his wrist, she lifted it until his watch was right under his nose. 'There's less than an hour,' she said, her scent wrapping around him in a seductive cloud. 'And I've a few things I'd like you to do.'

He groaned. 'Not rearrange the buffet tables...*again*?'

Her eyes were sparkling with mischief as they met his. 'Nothing *that* strenuous, but I'd hate for us to run short of ice for the drinks.'

Craig's pulse went into overdrive. 'Mel,' he said, steering his wife to the door, 'finish *wrapping things up* down here. Your mother needs me to check the bar.'

The teenager sent him a comprehending grin. 'Sure, Dad.'

When the door closed behind their departing parents, Summer shook her head. 'They must think we're pathetically naïve.'

'Yeah,' Mel said, raising an eyebrow. 'But not for much longer.'

Exchanging a meaningful glance, both girls erupted in laughter.

'So,' Taylor said, as she walked arm in arm with Craig towards their bedroom, 'are you going to deny you told Summer to take me on a wild-goose chase to keep me busy while you wrapped my gift?'

'Yep. That was Melanie's idea. I just asked them to *occupy* you.'

'Be more specific next time. I'm not exaggerating when I say we covered nearly every room from attic to cellar three times trying to "find" you.'

'I hope all that exertion hasn't tired you out,' he said with concern as he opened the door and gallantly stood back so she could enter ahead of him. 'Maybe an elevator would have been a good gift for you? What with your age and all...?'

'Watch it, Mr Adams.'

'*Oh, I am, Mrs Adams*! And believe me, lady, you still have the best-looking ass I've ever seen.' In a single motion, he hauled her into his arms, kicked the door shut and began kissing her.

It never ceased to amaze Taylor that even after all these years this man could still ignite her with a mere look. The taste, the feel of him just seemed to get better and better and her love for him grew deeper and stronger with every passing day. And the flames burning through her as they hungrily disposed of each other's clothing were equally hot and wild as they'd been when she was eighteen.

'Darling Tay, I love you.' The words came as he swept her into his arms and carried her to their bed. And they fell as one onto—

'Ouch! What the—?'

Breaking apart, they looked down at the silver-wrapped package that had intruded so rudely on their passion.

'I thought we agreed to exchange gifts tonight?' Craig said, picking it up.

'We did.' She smiled. 'This must be from one of the girls. Quick, open it up!'

Craig's eyes lowered to his lap. '*Now*?'

She chuckled. 'I know you. You'll keep.'

'And *you'll* be the death of me, Taylor Adams,' he muttered, ripping the paper off. 'Oh, my God!' he gasped.

'What is—? *Oh, my God!*'

'I believe I just said that, darling,' he returned, staring at the solid silver ice tray in his hands until Taylor snatched it from him.

He watched as a series of puzzled expressions crossed her face, and, not wanting her to assume the girls knew more than they should, he explained how Mel, when she was about Summer's age now, had been curious as to why there was often an ice tray in their bedroom and that he'd told her it was because Taylor's knee ached. The woman beside him burst out laughing.

'Well, hell, Taylor, it was all I could think of on the spur of the moment! Besides, I'm sure she bought it.'

'Yeah, right! Which is why *both* she and Summer giggled when *I* told them I'd tell them each on their wedding days,' she said, tears of amusement streaming down her face.

'You mean...they *guessed*? Damn! How could a couple of innocent little girls come up with—?'

Taylor's burst of hysterical giggles cut him off. 'Honey,' she said when she'd sobered enough to speak, 'I think it's about time you accepted that your innocent little daughters have grown into two very mature, well-adjusted young ladies who have their father's risqué sense of humour.' She smiled at his confused expression. 'Take a look at the inscription on the back.'

Turning the ice tray over, he read:

Happy 25th Anniversary, Mum & Dad
We love you, Melanie Brooke & Summer Jayne
Note: This is a hot *ice tray!*

Laughing fit to burst, he flopped back onto the bed next to his wife. 'I swear they're completely and utterly incorrigible!'

'They get that from you, too.'

'Ah, but they're also adorable.'

She grinned. 'Definitely my input.'

'Really?' Fighting his amusement, he propped himself up on one elbow. 'And whose genetic input accounts for the fact they're also loving and giving and—?'

She cupped his face in her hands, her eyes serious. 'They have those traits because they've grown up in a secure home where trust and love are valued more than anything else. *You* made that possible by being a wonderful husband and father, Craig Adams, and I'll love you forever.'

Her words flooded him with emotion. Every day this woman filled him with more love and pride than he'd ever imagined it was possible to feel. He brushed a gentle finger across her cheek. 'You, Tay, must be specially blessed by God.'

'I am,' she whispered confidently, drawing his head nearer. 'He gave me you.'

HARLEQUIN PRESENTS®

Psst. Pass it on...Harlequin Presents' exciting new miniseries is here!

Scandals!

You won't want to miss these scintillating stories of surprising affairs:

We've got your calendar booked!

Available wherever Harlequin books are sold.

HARLEQUIN WOMEN KNOW ROMANCE WHEN THEY SEE IT.

And they'll see it on **ROMANCE CLASSICS**, the new 24-hour TV channel devoted to romantic movies and original programs like the special **Harlequin** Showcase of Authors & Stories.

The **Harlequin** Showcase of Authors & Stories introduces you to many of your favorite romance authors in a program developed exclusively for Harlequin readers.

Watch for the **Harlequin** Showcase of Authors & Stories series beginning in the summer of 1997.

If you're not receiving ROMANCE CLASSICS, call your local cable operator or satellite provider and ask for it today!

Escape to the network of your dreams.

HARLEQUIN PRESENTS®

Coming in September...

~~Breaking~~ Making Up

by
Miranda Lee and
Susan Napier

Two original stories in one unique volume—
"Two for the price of one!"

Meet two irresistible men from
Down Under— one Aussie, one Kiwi.
The time has come for them to settle old scores
and win the women they've always wanted!

Look for ~~Breaking~~ *Making Up* (#1907)
in September 1997.

Available wherever Harlequin books are sold.